Mr. Pudgins

By Ruth Christoffer Carlsen

Illustrations by Margaret Bradfield

SCHOLASTIC BOOK SERVICES
NEW YORK · TORONTO · LONDON · AUCKLAND · SYDNEY · TOKYO

ISBN: 0-590-01339-4

21 20 19 18 17 16 15 14 13 12 11 10   9/7 01/8

Printed in the U.S.A.

To
CHRISTOPHER, KRISTIN, *and* PETER
who alone know how many
of these adventures
really happened

Contents

1. Mr. Pudgins

My mother is a very particular woman, and that's how we got Mr. Pudgins. There are three of us children. I'm John, the oldest. Then there's Janey, who is six, with her hair in pigtails and her front teeth missing. And last there's Pete, just four, a round, chunky kid with a big grin and lots of bounce. I'm positive I could take care of the others, but Mother always insists that we have a babysitter just in case we have an emergency — which we never do.

This time all the old familiar babysitters were busy. I guess January is a busy month. And Mother and Dad just had to go to this dinner. So Mother called Mrs. Henry, who runs the grocery store, and she knew of Mr. Pudgins. "He's a pleasant little man and seems very responsible. You should see the pickles and rye bread that he buys here," she said with a laugh.

1

Mother wasn't very eager to try him, but she finally had to. Pete and I were rather pleased. We had never had a man before. So on this Thursday night we all three of us stood at the windows and watched. Suddenly we heard an awful noise, like a concrete mixer

with whooping cough. A cloud of dust rolled down the street, and when it blew away, there sat the oldest car we had ever seen. Maybe it was the very first Model-T Ford.

"An old-fashioned car," squealed Petey.

Janey and I laughed. And then out climbed a round button of a man. For a moment all we saw was ears and nose. Then he smiled and waved at us, and his eyes made us feel good all over. He was puffing on his pipe, and there was so much smoke that he walked to the door in a cloud.

"Dear me, a pipe," said Mother weakly as she opened the door.

"I am Mr. Pudgins," said a deep voice, and he stepped out of the smoke into the living room.

Petey started to yell, "I got a new puzzle. Come see my puzzle."

"No! No!" screamed Janey. "I want him to play dolls."

"Oh, goodness, children," said Mother, "please, please, be good." Then she gave Mr. Pudgins some instructions about putting us to bed, and she and Dad left.

"May we have a ride in your car?" I asked.

"My, no," said Mr. Pudgins. "Annabelle is not feeling at all well. Didn't you hear her coughing as I drove up?"

"Annabelle? Is that the car's name?" asked Janey.

"Annabelle it is," he answered. "And now to bed."

Usually Janey and Pete put up an awful fuss with new babysitters. They really do test them, and I was wondering what would happen to Mr. Pudgins. But before I could say the names of all my model planes, Janey was tucked in with her blanket and dolls, Peter had his drink and bear and was snug in bed, and Mr. Pudgins was studying the directions of my latest model plane. We had just started to work with the glue when, all of a sudden, we heard a little girl's voice. "OOOooohhhhh . . ." Gosh, it was a terrific wail!

"What's the matter, Janey?" called Mr. Pudgins.

"There's a bear in here."

"You can't believe her, Mr. Pudgins," I put in. "She's always imagining things."

"I always believe a child," said Mr. Pudgins almost crossly. "If she says there's a bear, then there's probably a bear."

"Hurry! It's right on my dresser." Janey was screaming now.

I couldn't help snickering, but I followed him into the bedroom. When he turned on the light, I was all ready to say, "I told you so." But, jumping jelly beans, there was a bear on the dresser! A big brown bear, too, and it looked mighty cross. So did Mr. Pudgins, who was holding Janey. The bear growled low and nastily. I jumped a little closer to Mr. Pudgins, and just then I felt someone pull at my p.j.'s. There was Pete. "Look, look! He's lost from the circus," yipped Pete.

"He most certainly is not," said Mr. Pudgins in a very positive tone.

"How can you be so sure?" I asked.

"He just said so," answered Mr. Pudgins.

We all stared at him. "You mean . . . ?"

"Oh, of course, I can understand him," said Mr. Pudgins. "He wants to know who made him materialize?"

"What's that mean?" quavered Janey.

"Arrive, show up, become alive." Mr. Pudgins

sounded quite put out as if he didn't approve of bears
arriving.

"You mean we did it?" yelled Pete, really excited
now. "Oh, let's get a lion. I want a lion."

"One bear is quite enough, young man," said Mr.
Pudgins. "Now what are we going to do with it?"

The bear started walking around the dresser top, but

there wasn't much room, and after he turned around and about and around again, he growled.

"I can't help it," said Mr. Pudgins, as if he were answering the bear.

"What did he say?"

"He simply said it was very inconvenient to be called here when he was right in the middle of his long winter nap."

"What's his name?" whispered Janey.

The bear garumphed, and Mr. Pudgins said, "Umdahl."

"That's no name," Petey said.

"The bear seems to like it," said Mr. Pudgins. Right then Umdahl jumped down and began snuffling under the bed. Janey began screaming, and this time she opened up like a fire engine. Up and down the scale she went. The noise was terrific. Umdahl lay down, put his paws over his ears, and moaned. Mr. Pudgins said, "Stop that noise this minute."

And she did. Then there was only Umdahl's groaning. "What's the matter with him?" shouted Pete. He seemed to think our sitter was deaf.

"He's hungry."

"Let's feed him. Let's feed him," yelled Pete.

"What in the world will we feed a bear?" I asked. I knew Mom wouldn't want any missing roasts in the morning.

"Marshmallows," said Janey in a positive tone.

The bear garumphed, and Mr. Pudgins said, "She's absolutely right. It's marshmallows he wants."

We made a parade into the kitchen. First, Mr. Pudgins with Janey right behind, then Umdahl next with Pete on his back, and then me. I kept wishing the kids at school could see me. Only I knew they wouldn't believe it. Imagine a real live bear in our kitchen!

Umdahl sat down on top of the stove. He growled at Mr. Pudgins, who still seemed very put out at his appearance. "I don't understand it," he muttered as he rummaged about in the cupboard. "I simply don't understand it."

He tore open the marshmallow package, and then Peter and Janey started screeching and throwing the marshmallows at Umdahl, who caught them with his paws, his nose, his tongue. It was better than a circus. I threw one that went up to the ceiling, and Umdahl almost jumped off the stove to get it. When he came down on his claws, there was a ripping noise, like chalk on the blackboard, and sure enough, there was a bad scratch on the stove. I hoped Mother wouldn't ask me how it got there.

Suddenly, oh much too suddenly, the marshmallows were all gone, and Umdahl started licking his fur like a big cat. I wondered if he were going to settle down for the winter with us, right there on the stove.

"Please, Mr. Pudgins," begged Janey. "Let me ride him. Make him get down so I can ride him."

"He'd better get off Mom's stove," I added.

Mr. Pudgins grabbed Umdahl by the fur and started pulling. Nothing happened, except Umdahl looked surprised and not at all pleased. So I grabbed Mr. Pudgins around the middle, and we both pulled. Still nothing happened. Janey pulled on me, and Pete pulled on her, and the four of us tugged and groaned. Whurrrumph! Umdahl snarled and growled like a

steam engine getting under way. He blew the four of us right across the floor and in a heap.

"That," said Mr. Pudgins, "is definitely the wrong approach." So the four of us sat and thought.

Janey started rubbing her eyes and yawning. "I don't want to sit here all night. I want to go to bed."

"Do go then," said Mr. Pudgins with his head in his hands, thinking.

"But I want to be put to bed right." I could tell from the way her face was puckering that she was going to cry. And she did. It was her fire-engine wail again.

Peter opened up and joined her. Mr. Pudgins looked surprised, and Umdahl put his paws over his ears and moaned.

"Stop it! All three of you!" said Mr. Pudgins in a positive voice.

And they did. All three of them. He had a gleam in his eye as he said to Janey, "What is the right way to go to bed?"

I could see her settling down to explain. "Well, first I have to have my drink."

"Yes?"

"And then I get my pink blanket and my baby . . ."

"Yes?"

"Then after I get in bed, I say my prayers. . . ."

"Yes, yes?"

"And my mommy or daddy gives me a big bear hug."

"Bear hug! Bear hug!" shrieked Mr. Pudgins, jumping to his feet. "That's it."

Umdahl suddenly jumped down from the stove and began walking around and around us. Janey looked frightened. "Does he have to hug me?" she whispered, nodding at Umdahl. "He's so big."

Mr. Pudgins asked him, and Umdahl growled. "It's some kind of a bear custom, he says," explained Mr. Pudgins. "It's the only thing that will send him back. He'll be very careful."

So we all got in line again, and back to the bedroom we marched. After Janey was tucked in bed and the lights turned out, all we could see were Umdahl's green eyes like two small headlights. Then he walked toward Janey's bed. I thought surely she'd scream. I was so worried myself that I wanted to yelp. There was a swish, a murmur from Janey, and then the lights disappeared. Mr. Pudgins turned the light switch and Umdahl was gone.

"He's gone," wailed Petey.

"Thank heavens," said Mr. Pudgins as he picked Peter up and turned the light off. "And if I were you," he said as he went out the door, "I should not say a word of this in the morning to anyone. Not one word, mind you. It had better be our secret."

It was. For in the morning, as I tripped on my shoelace coming down the hall to breakfast, I heard Mom say to Dad in an exasperated voice, "Honestly, Jack, look at this kitchen. A marshmallow on the ceiling, a scratch on my stove. Look, all the marshmallows are gone."

"Maybe they had a free-for-all last night with the marshmallows," came Dad's voice. "We used to do that in college."

"Humph," said Mother. "They're a little young to be starting that. It's a wonder they aren't all sick. I've a good notion to give that Mr. Pudgins a piece of my mind. Letting them eat a whole pound of marshmallows. And this scratch. It would take something sharp to make such a gouge."

Quietly I crept back down the hall. No use seeing Mom and Dad now. Let 'em speculate. Gollee. I wouldn't dare tell them what really happened. Besides, it was too slumgumptious a tale to share with someone as old as our folks.

2. Mr. Pudgins and the Mirror Children

It was one of those bad afternoons. Outside, the sidewalks were thick with the slush of a February thaw. Dad was out of town, and Mother had gone to a party in the country. Fortunately, we had been able to persuade Mother to let us have Mr. Pudgins babysit. She was still pretty provoked about the marshmallows and the scratch on her stove, but by Janey's crying, Pete's smiling, and my begging, we'd won her over.

My friends were all off visiting grandmothers or friends or downtown. Janey had the sniffles, and Mother insisted she stay in until it was dry outside. And Pete always did what Janey did. So there were the three of us and Mr. Pudgins with nothing to do and nobody with an idea. Janey and Pete were standing

with their noses against the big long mirror in the hall.
"I wish," said Janey, "that the little girl in the mirror
could come out to play."

"Me too," chimed in Pete.

"Because," said Janey, "if she could come and play,
she'd be just the right age for me." The idea sounded
pretty interesting, so I went and looked in too. And, of
course, there were three children looking out at us.

Just at that moment Petey banged his head against
the mirror, and a strange voice said, "Ouch."

We all looked at each other, and then we looked at
Mr. Pudgins, who was sitting in his favorite easy chair,
smoking his pipe. Strange things always seemed to
happen when he was smoking that pipe. "Did you say
'ouch,' Mr. Pudgins?" asked Janey.

"Why in the world would I say 'ouch'?" he replied.

"But somebody did," said Janey.

"I said 'ow,'" said Pete.

"Well, 'ow' and 'ouch' are two different words," I said
with the authority of being the oldest. Then we looked
back in the mirror as Petey rubbed his head. The little
boy in the mirror was rubbing his head, too. I thought
for a moment, and then went up and hit that boy like
me in the stomach.

"Hey, cut that out!" said another voice. I grinned.

"Come on out of there, dopey, or I'll hit you again," I
said in a fierce voice.

"All right, all right. You don't need to be nasty. Give me a pull."

I did, and out of the mirror stepped the boy. He looked like me, he talked like me, but he didn't walk like me. He floated. I grabbed his hand and said, "Hey, stay down here!"

"Okay," said the other boy. "Though it is nice just to drift about."

"Oh," squealed Janey. "Oh, oh, oh. I want my little girl, too. Come on, little girl." And sure enough, Janey pulled the little girl right out of the mirror.

"Come on," yelled Pete as he yanked his mirror boy out of the frame. The three of us looked at the three of them, and they looked back at us. We had to hold on to them tightly, though, or they would have floated right up to the ceiling.

"What's your name?" said Janey. Girls always start a conversation that way.

"Mirjaney," said the new little girl.

"Mine's Janey. They're sort of alike," said Janey.

"My name's Mirpete," said the littler boy.

"And mine's Mirjohn," said my friend.

"Hey!" I was suddenly struck with an idea. "Our names are just alike, except theirs have a Mir in front of them." I thought some more. "I suppose that's because they're mirror children." I was pretty pleased that I had figured that out.

"Let's play a game," said Janey.

"Hurray! Hurray!" we all shouted.

"I know," said I. "Let's play ball on our backs. The mirror children can lie on their backs on the ceiling, and we'll lie on our backs on the floor. Then we can throw the ball up and down to each other."

All three of us lay flat on the floor and all three of them floated up to the ceiling. Wham! Wham! The ball went back and forth. It was bad when they missed because sometimes the ball left a mark on the ceiling. Mr. Pudgins suggested we had better play some other

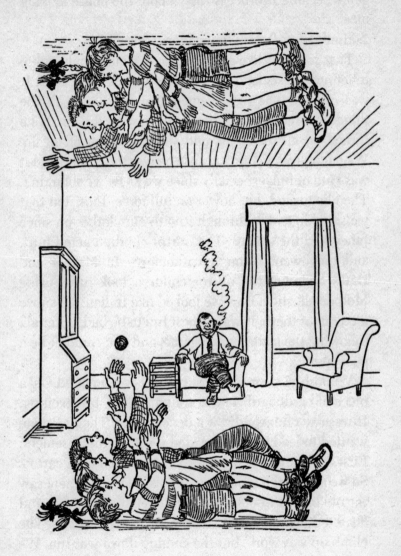

game because Mother is fussy about the house looking nice.

"Let's play follow-the-leader," said Pete.

That sounded like a good idea. It seemed only polite to let our guests lead off, so Mirjohn was the leader. It was odd, but he just seemed bent on doing all the things we had always been told not to do. First, he turned on all the lights and snapped them off again. We had to follow him because he was the leader, and it was kind of fun, especially since we knew we shouldn't. Then he turned the shower on full force. I insisted that we shouldn't walk through it with our clothes on since Janey had the sniffles. The mirror children acted hurt, and they went through without us. In Mother and Dad's bedroom the mirror children took turns using Mother's lipstick. Boy, we looked like Indians when we filed out of there. It was almost fun to be bad. After all, following the leader was a game, and you couldn't be a poor sport.

Whoosh! Down the front stairs we bumped on a piece of cardboard. It was rough sliding, but exciting. It was such fun we did it a dozen times. Then Mirpete wanted to lead, and he headed right for the basement. First, he grabbed a hammer and pounded on a carton. So we all did the same. It was noisy. Then Mirpete saw the old brown wooden icebox and climbed up that and floated down. It wasn't so easy for the three of us. The climb up was work, but the coming down was fun. We kept that up until Mr. Pudgins' voice called, "Children, not so much noise."

Then we acted very quiet. We crept around the basement on our hands and knees, pretending we were bears or dogs or cows or monkeys. Finally, Mirpete pretended he was a frog and jumped in Mother's new automatic washing machine. That was bad, because Mirjaney flipped the switch and the machine started. Around and around it whirled Mirpete while we struggled with the switch. It wouldn't snap to "off." Finally, I pulled the cord and the motor stopped. Mirpete couldn't stand up when he got out. He couldn't float off. He was so dizzy that he just kept turning around

and around. I decided we'd better not stay in the basement. We were all pretty tired anyway, so we trooped upstairs to the kitchen.

"What'll we do now, Mr. Pudgins?" I asked.

"Are you hungry?"

Until he mentioned it, I hadn't realized how hungry I really was. "Oh, boy! I'll say I am."

"How about some popcorn?" said Mr. Pudgins.

That was a wonderful idea. I got out our electric popper and the ten-pound can of popcorn which Mother always buys because she says it's more economical. And we set to work. The first batch certainly hit the spot. We decided to make some more. "Here," I said, "you mirror children make popcorn while we go downstairs to get some root beer. Come on, Pete and Jane."

And then it happened. Petey dropped a big bottle of root beer he was carrying on the basement floor, and the root beer went everywhere. There was only one thing to do: clean up the mess. Janey picked up glass, Petey wiped the walls, and I mopped at the root beer. It took a long time to get it looking neat again. Then we picked up our bottles and started up the stairs. When we stepped into the kitchen, we stopped short. There was popcorn in the dishpan. There was popcorn in every pan and kettle. There was popcorn piled high everywhere.

"Got a good batch started in the bathtub, too," said Mirpete.

"Jumping jiminy," I shouted. "Why didn't you stop?"

"You said, 'Make popcorn while we're gone.' Well, you just got back," said Mirjohn. "We're making popcorn."

"Oh, gosh! Oh, jiminy! Now what'll we do? Turn off that thing."

Janey ran to pull the plug out, and it wouldn't budge. We emptied another batch of popcorn in the bathtub. There was no doubt about it, it was about to overflow.

"Mr. Pudgins," yelled Pete. "Help, Mr. Pudgins!"

Mr. Pudgins' pipe and nose came around the door and then Mr. Pudgins. He looked surprised. "Isn't that enough popcorn, John?"

"Can't you stop it?" I begged.

So all seven of us pulled on the cord, and whooey blam! We slid across the floor when the plug broke loose. The popcorn popper was stopped, but what were we to do with the popcorn?

"We'll have to sell it," I moaned.

"Oh, goody, goody," said Janey who loves to go around to the neighbors.

"We'll have to be going now," said Mirjohn.

"Hey, you help us clean up the mess," I shouted.

"Good-bye," they whispered, and all three floated past us and right into the mirror. I rushed over and tried to argue with Mirjohnny, but there's no use trying to talk to a hunk of glass, especially when the other fellow does just the same things you're doing. I gave up.

"Get on your bike, Johnny, and go down to the grocery store. Buy ten dozen bags of assorted sizes," said Mr. Pudgins.

I was back in a jiffy, though I know Mrs. Henry, our grocer's wife, was surprised at that order. We salted and buttered the great mass of corn — humps and hills and mountains of popcorn. Then we packed it in the bags, loaded the bags on the wagon, and set off to sell the stuff. It was twilight when we were through. Mr. Pudgins had cleaned up the kitchen, and I was relieved. Honestly, we were all too tired to do more than wiggle our little fingers.

Mother was surprised when she got home to find us already in bed. She was even more surprised when she heard that we had been out selling popcorn. "How ever do you think of these things, Mr. Pudgins?" she asked. "And to think they made a profit of five dollars and sixty cents. What a constructive idea!"

I wanted to tell her that there was nothing constructive about it. We had had to work our way out of a mess. But then, maybe it was better to let Mother think we had been constructive. So I drifted off to sleep, and all that night I climbed little hills, big hills, and mountains of popcorn.

3. Mr. Pudgins and the Whizzle

Wʜᴀᴛ ᴄᴀɴ you do on a rainy afternoon? It had been raining for days, and we had used up all of our ideas. We were tired of rain. Gosh! It would come during spring vacation, too. Mother and Dad were off buying spring clothes. They just always had to get new outfits for themselves and everybody else when spring vacation rolled around. It's a wonder they didn't buy a suit for the Easter bunny.

Peter was standing with his nose pressed against the window waiting for the rain to stop. But it didn't. Janey was dressing her Coo doll for the umpteenth time, and I was fiddling with the propeller on a new model plane. Mr. Pudgins was playing a game of solitaire. He looked mighty bored. We all were.

"Let's have a tea party. Can't we, Mr. Pudgins?" Janey stood in front of him with a smile on her face. The two missing teeth made her grin look like a pumpkin's.

"Capital idea, my dear. Capital. Give me a hand to get out of this deep chair." Mr. Pudgins was so rolypoly that Janey had to tug to get him out. "What will it be, children?"

"I want some Whizzle," said Pete.

"Whizzle?" said Mr. Pudgins.

"Oh yes, some Whizzle," said Janey.

"What in the world is Whizzle, Johnny?" Mr. Pudgins turned toward me. He took his pipe out of his pocket, and I felt goose pimples all over.

"Well, Johnny?" asked Mr. Pudgins.

"Gosh, don't ask me. It must be something they made up."

"Does anybody know what goes into it?" asked Mr. Pudgins, striking a match to light his pipe.

"Ginger ale, 'cause that makes it whiz," said Pete.

"You mean fizz, Pete," I said. "There's no such drink."

"It seems to me my grandfather told me of a very interesting drink called Whizzle. Just the thing for an afternoon like this," said Mr. Pudgins. "You youngsters go and wash your hands. And I'll get to work in the kitchen."

When he brought in the pitcher, it was filled to the top with a dark-red mixture that bubbled like a fountain. We each took a sip of the Whizzle.

"That's good," said Pete.

"Mmmmmm, Whizzle," said Janey.

"Not bad, not bad," said I.

It really did taste good. There was cherry juice, orange juice, ginger ale, and then a flavor I couldn't figure out, all mixed up together. Each of us drank a tall glassful. Then we drank another. Even Mr. Pudgins was enjoying his concoction.

Just as we emptied our glasses, Peter had a terrific burp. It almost knocked him off his chair. "Burrrrppppee — wow!" And when he said that wow, out of his mouth flew a bird. Not a very big bird, to be sure, but a bird just the same. It was reddish in color and quick in its movements.

"For goodness sakes," said Janey.

Then she burped. It was catching, I guess. Ooops, a bird flew out of her mouth, but orange in color.

"Mine's prettier," said Janey with pride as the bird flew up and sat on Mother's new lamp.

I felt a burp coming, a big burp. I tried to hold it in and then, "Whoooeeka-burp!" There was a green bird sitting on my finger. He looked surprised, and so was I. All three of us looked at Mr. Pudgins then. He was laughing, and then it came. The biggest burp of all. "Blooooey-burp!" And a big, red, green, and blue bird flew out.

The four birds started to fly round and round, singing as they went. But we were in trouble. That first
burp started us hiccupping, and once we had started,
we couldn't seem to stop. With each hiccup another
bird flew out. There were birds here, birds there, big
and little birds everywhere.

"Hold your nose. Hup, hup, hic!" said Mr. Pudgins
and hiccupped two more birds.

"Stand on your right foot." Petey got mixed up and
stood on his left.

"Shut your eyes. Hup, hic-hup." Three birds flew out.

"Now jump on your right foot and hold your breath."

All four of us jumped. Janey turned white, Petey turned purple, but Mr. Pudgins turned red.

"Whooof!" I gasped, and so did the others when we gulped air again. Yes, the hiccups had stopped.

"Hic!" We all turned and looked. Petey was very unhappy. He hadn't stopped hiccupping. Another bird flew into the room. And those birds here, birds there, big and little birds everywhere were getting in our hair, Mother's draperies, the cookie jar, the bathtub. It was terrible. Mr. Pudgins grabbed Petey by the feet and swung him upside down. But with each swing he hiccupped some more. Janey ran and got a fierce skeleton

mask we'd had for Halloween and pounced on Petey
trying to scare the hiccups away. But Pete just kept on
hiccupping.

"We've got to stop him," I moaned.

"Now let me see," said Mr. Pudgins. "He doesn't
scare and he doesn't bounce . . ."

"Let's put him outside," said Janey. "I'm getting
tired of birds."

"But it's raining," wailed Petey, and he started to
kick and yell. That did it. Suddenly we realized he had
stopped hiccupping.

"That solved that," said Mr. Pudgins. "But what are we to do with these birds?" What a problem!

"Let's keep them," said Petey. He always had an easy solution.

"I want to catch them," said Janey.

"Say," I said, "Mother will be mad if she finds all these birds flying around. Come on, we'd better get them outdoors."

"Johnny is right," said Mr. Pudgins. "Now let me see: Johnny, you get the vacuum sweeper and put on the attachment that sucks up air. That shouldn't hurt the littler ones. Janey, you get the old bird cage in the basement and catch them in that. And Petey and I will take big pans with covers and catch them in those. All set? Let's go."

It was lucky no one walked in on us during the next half-hour, for there was I pulling the vacuum sweeper after me and sticking the hose in the draperies, on the lamps, over the doors, under the ventilators and sucking in dozens and dozens of birds. Janey was hopping up and down on the chairs, the sink, the shelves, the shower, and catching dozens and dozens of birds in her cage. And Mr. Pudgins and Petey were making an awful racket slamming the covers on their pans after they'd caught another bird. We raced here and there and everywhere. At last the big birds, little birds, red birds, green birds were all caught and thrown outside. We all sat down in chairs and panted. Then we looked at the room. It was a mess. Lampshade knocked sideways, draperies pulled every which way, dirt on chairs, windows smeared, the carpet littered.

"H'um," said Mr. Pudgins, "I know what we'll do next."

"So do I," said Janey weakly. And so did we all. We had to clean up the house.

Peter straightened all the things that had been knocked awry, Janey dusted, Mr. Pudgins washed windows, and I vacuumed. Boy, we were tired when that was done! We were just putting away the last rag and the vacuum sweeper when we heard Mother's key in the lock.

"Gosh!" I muttered. "We just made it."

"What a lovely surprise," said Mother as she walked in the door. "What a lovely clean house." She turned to Mr. Pudgins. "How in the world do you do it?" she asked. Mr. Pudgins just smiled, rather weakly, I think.

"Hey," said Dad, coming through the door with a load of packages, "where did that pretty green canary come from?"

We all gasped. Sure enough, there was one of the birds. We must have missed him. "Get the cage and catch him, Petey," said Mother.

"Oh no, Mommy," wailed Petey. "I'm tired of catching them. You catch it. Please, Mommy." So she did.

"What shall we call our new bird?" asked Mother as she hung the cage in a sunny window.

"I know," said Janey. "Whizzle." And we did. But never again on a rainy afternoon did we ask for a party with Whizzle. Once was enough.

4. Podo, the Dodo Bird

MOTHER was a Mary. Grandma was a Mary. A great aunt and three cousins were Marys. Every May they had a gathering of the Marys, and Mother explained to Dad that it was just a must. She had to go. This was the afternoon that she was off being Mary, as Dad jokingly called it, so Mr. Pudgins was with us.

It was a swell day.

I was almost ready to go to Clem's to practice shooting balls at his basket. It was just the kind of spring day for basketball. And then Petey started his fuss. "Where's my hammer?" he yelled. And I remembered I had used it last.

Mr. Pudgins was sitting reading the newspaper, and smoke billowed over its edges. "Do you know where the hammer is, Johnny?" he asked.

37

Oh dear! I knew what that meant. I was going to have to stop and look for that hammer. "No," I grumbled. "But I suppose I'll have to look for it." We looked under the work bench, all through the toolbox, and even in the garage. I was getting cross. Even if I had used it, I couldn't see that it was my fault it had mysteriously disappeared.

"There's a hammer in Annabelle," said Mr. Pudgins nodding toward the door. "In the trunk. You can use that one, Pete."

Peter ran outside, and in a minute had his head inside that high old trunk, for Mr. Pudgins' car was a Model-T coupe. It was a mighty interesting car. I was watching him as I pulled my sweat shirt over my head to leave,

and then I gasped. "Hey, Mr. Pudgins! Pete's blowing away!"

Janey rushed from the bedroom, Mr. Pudgins jumped from his armchair, and I started for the door. Just at that minute, Pete blew by at window level. He seemed to be turning somersaults lazily as he went by. And right ahead of him was a queer-looking thing. I only got a glimpse, so I couldn't tell if it was a bird, animal, or piece of paper.

We all rushed outside, and just as we rounded the corner of the house that same blast of air caught us. Up into the air we flew and then blew along after Pete. He was halfway down the block. I could hear Mr. Pudgins puffing and exclaiming, and then, up-si-daisy, I was turning slowly over. It was disconcerting. I struggled to get my feet back to the ground, but the air resisted my efforts. Janey was giggling, and when I looked back she was higher than the rest of us. "Paddle," yelled Mr. Pudgins. So I paddled with my hands and began to gain on Pete. In front of McClotsky's I grabbed Pete's leg.

"Let go," he screamed.

"Don't be crazy. I've been trying to catch you!"

"But I have to catch that thing. It flew out of the car. I've got to catch it."

"Paddle then," I yelled. But just as I yelled that, Mr. Pudgins sailed by me, and with one mighty push grabbed the thing. As soon as he touched it, the wind went down, and we all went boomp, landing right flat on the grass! It was lucky we weren't over the sidewalk. Janey came running up.

"What happened to the wind? I want to fly!"

Mr. Pudgins wasn't paying any attention to her. He was shaking a queer-looking bird. It was something like a turkey in size, but its wings were so tiny that they were of no use at all. And it had a horn-shaped nose that looked as if it had been squashed together by someone pushing too hard on it.

"What a funny little fluff of a tail. Is it really a tail?" Janey was pointing at some feathers that stuck up.

"Of course," said Mr. Pudgins. "Of course it's a tail. But Podo was very naughty. He deserves a spanking."

"What is it?" I asked.

Mr. Pudgins acted rather cross as we started walking back home. "A dodo bird. Podo is a dodo bird. Surely, you've heard of those."

"But they're extinct."

"Does that mean they smell?" shouted Petey, who was running after us. Mr. Pudgins was just striding along.

"Oh, don't be dumb. Extinct means none left . . . dead . . . gone." I glared at Petey.

"He's not dead," said Petey.

"He's cute," said Janey. "But I'd like that wind again."

"No more wind," said Mr. Pudgins firmly. "You can see that a dodo bird has such small wings it can't fly. So when Podo wants to fly, he just sucks in air, blows it out that horn of a nose, hops on the wind, and blows along. It's a nuisance." He gave the dodo another shake. "I ought to send him back where he came from."

The dodo bird hung its head.

"Where did he come from?" asked Janey as we turned up our walk.

But Mr. Pudgins didn't answer her. "Come," he said, "let's sit out on the back lawn where we can just talk."

"Does it talk?" gasped Petey.

"Of course I talk," said Podo with a loud nasal twang.

"Oh, he does. He does," squealed Janey, pulling up a chair and looking intently at the dodo.

"But I don't like your language," said the dodo.

Mr. Pudgins set the dodo down on the grass, and the bird waddled around looking us over. "Queer-looking things you are, aren't you? No feathers . . ." He nipped at my arms. "Useless-looking wings."

"They aren't wings," I said.

"What are those flaps sticking out from your head? Are they wings?" The dodo was staring at me.

"Oh, those are ears. I hear with them," I grumbled.

"They certainly are queer," said the dodo.

"Not any queerer than you."

The dodo just said, "Hummph."

"Now, children," said Mr. Pudgins as he pulled out his pipe and began to puff. "No quarreling. Why don't you, Podo, say a poem for us in your dodo language?"

"Oh, may I?" said Podo, bouncing up and down. "Oh, joy!"

He pulled a few feathers in place, bounced his tail until it fluffed out a bit, and then sang in his voice like a locomotive whistle:

Glibbitty, bobbity, sibbidy, dobbidy,
Ibbidy, jibbidy, sobbidy, nobbidy . . .
Hurrahbidy, hurrahbidy, hurrahbidy, hurrah,
Mirrabidy, gurrahbidy, currahbidy, gurrah.

Petey started to laugh, and even Mr. Pudgins was smiling. The dodo bird got very huffy. "It is not a funny song," he said. "It is a song in praise of the sun and flowers."

"It doesn't sound like it," said Janey.

"It does too," growled the dodo, and a big tear ran down his short crushed nose. "That's just what it does. You may not understand the words, but the sound, the feeling, should reach through to you."

"Oh, dear. Now you've hurt his feelings," said Mr. Pudgins. "Come, come, Podo. They didn't mean it. Perhaps they'd like to learn to talk just like you."

"I can do it now," I said, jumping to my feet.

> In the scabbayshous, layshous, bracious
> I can maysheous my calayshous
> And the nashous, hateful glayshous
> Will drop stinkshous on my rayshous.

"How's that?" I grinned. The dodo bird looked rather doubtful. "I'm not sure that's a very happy song," he said, "but it's not bad."

"It's my turn now," said Janey. "I've got a dodo poem, too."

> Heffala, heffala, heffala kanoba.
> Treffala, treffala in the groba.
> Whoofink, whoofink, on the wattink.
> Listen to the muffler batink.

Petey clapped his hands. "Me now. Me."

The dodo was sitting back on his bit of a tail, and tears were running down his cheeks. "Come, come, Podo, don't be so sad," said Mr. Pudgins.

"But it is so sad," said Podo wailing. "Those poor little mufflers batinking and batinking. I don't know if I can stand any more."

"Me, me!" shouted Pete.

"All right, Pete," said Mr. Pudgins. "Begin."

Pete looked around at us all and then just barely whispered:

> When the biffla comes and whifflas
> Then the sifflas run and griffla,
> But oh! the awful snicker snaffle
> When the giffers whicker whaffle.

"How's that? How's that?" shouted Pete, jumping up and down in excitement.

"Not bad, Pete. Not bad at all," said Mr. Pudgins. And then an awful noise ripped the air. It sounded almost like a fire siren crossed with a locomotive whistle. But it was only the dodo lying nose down and crying. He had a little pool of tears right at his feet.

"It's so sad," he sobbed. "So sad. Put me away. I can't stand any more."

"Now, now, Podo. I'll go and tuck you in Annabelle. We'll have the neighbors complaining if you keep wailing."

"Oh, jibbidy," I said.

"No whibbidy?" asked Janey. We started to giggle. And while Mr. Pudgins carried the wailing dodo bird off, we kept talking dodo talk.

"Will you sibbidy your rubbers?" I asked Jane.

"Not with my nose aglogga," she answered.

"Please, globbidy," said Pete.

"Oh, ruffidy, roddidy," said Jane.

And just then Mother came around the corner with Mr. Pudgins and stopped short when she saw us sitting on the chairs, waving our hands and talking. But she couldn't hear the talk.

"How do you do it?" I heard her murmur as she came up to us. "Imagine their sitting in the yard, just talking."

"Quite simple," said Mr. Pudgins, "if you know how."

"And I glibbidy the iddity," I added. But Mother just shook her head and wondered.

5. Mr. Pudgins Turns Plumber

Boy, THIS WAS a hot day even for July. I felt sorry for Dad, off being the rear end of a horse. His club was putting on a show and supper for the kids in the Crippled Children's Hospital, and that's the part Dad drew. Mother kept saying she thought a man of his intelligence at least ought to have been the front part, but Dad said he could be funnier where he was. I wished I could see him. Mother had to help serve the supper.

We were lucky, though, because Mr. Pudgins was staying with us, and you could never tell what might happen. I decided to build a stand to sell lemonade. I'd do a big business on a day like this. About the time I began pounding the board across the two orange crates, Janey and Pete came in from the back yard. They were a mess. I guess they had turned the hose into the garden and then dug in the mud. Mr. Pudgins took one look at them and said, "Bathtub for you two. Forward march."

And they marched, but right away the trouble began. I could hear the fuss in the bathroom. The cold water wouldn't run.

"Where's a wrench?" asked Mr. Pudgins, sticking his head out of the door and calling to me.

"You'd better call a plumber. Mother's written his name down on that little book on the telephone stand."

"Nonsense!" he answered. "I can handle this myself. Where's a wrench?"

I showed him where the wrench was, and he clumped down into the basement. Awful noises — banging, clanging, whooshing noises came out of the basement. Then Mr. Pudgins came upstairs looking very satisfied. "I guess that fixed it," he said, rubbing his hands together. "Is it all right, Janey?" he called.

We could hear the water running and excited squeals from the bathroom. "All's well," said Mr. Pudgins and sat down to smoke his pipe. "Might as well let them play awhile and cool off."

I had just finished the sign that said "Cold Drink 5¢" when I heard Mr. Pudgins say in a horrified voice, "For goodness sakes!" I ran into the house. Something was up.

When I saw Janey and Pete, I just stared. They were a pale purple all over — hair, cheeks, stomach, legs. Back and forth they paraded, as if they had a fancy costume on.

"What happened to them?" I gasped.

"I was wondering the same thing myself," said Mr. Pudgins. He got up, and we followed him to the bathroom. The tub was filled with some purple stuff.

"What's in that tub?" said Mr. Pudgins sternly.

"I don't know," said Janey. "It just whooshed right out of the faucet."

"Good to drink, too," said Petey.

I turned on the tap, and a purple liquid gushed out. I stuck my finger in the stuff and tasted it. "Ummmmm. It is good — grape pop."

Mr. Pudgins tried a bit and smiled. "Not bad at all."

"I'm going to run that into pitchers and sell it just like that. Boy, what luck! Try the washbowl, Janey."

And she did. Out came, not purple stuff, but orange. And that tasted like orange pop. In fact, it was orange pop. I almost knocked Petey down running to the kitchen. There the cold-water faucet ran lime pop. "Down to the basement, kids," I yelled. And we tore downstairs. Janey turned on the faucet in the washtub and out gushed a brown drink.

Pete tasted it and grinned. "Root beer," he yelled. "This is my place. I'm going to drink here."

"Everybody get a pitcher and fill it with a different pop," I shouted. "Watch our business grow." And away we tore. But Mr. Pudgins caught Petey and Jane, and made them put on sunsuits. They really attracted people. Everyone who walked by our house wanted to know how the youngsters got purple. So while we told them about the faucets in our house, they drank lots of glasses of root beer, orange pop, limeade, and grape pop. Business was wonderful.

Even some of the mothers came to buy our drinks by the quart. By then, though, Janey and Pete had disappeared, so the parents didn't get to see their new color. Dinner was certainly different, too. The potatoes had been boiled in orange pop, and they had a very

different flavor. For a change, Mr. Pudgins had cooked
the carrots in the limeade, and our lettuce had been
washed in the grape pop. Only the meat looked perfectly normal.

"Yummmm," said Petey. "I like these potatoes." He
hadn't eaten any potatoes for months, but he just dived
into those orange-colored ones.

"And I like the grape-pop salad," said Janey. "Lettuce and grape pop is delicious."

"Say, even these limeade carrots are good. I bet nobody in town is having a dinner like this," I said.

"I daresay you are absolutely right," said Mr. Pudgins, eating quietly and quickly. "Would you like some more root beer?" asked Mr. Pudgins. We had decided to have root beer as our drink, since there was no cold water. And to finish our meal we had cookies and popsicles, any flavor we wanted. We had made them from our pop. Oh, that was the best meal we had ever had. When it was over, though, Mr. Pudgins looked very thoughtful. "Now," he said, "I must go down in the basement and see just what I did wrong."

"Oh no, Mr. Pudgins," begged Janey, "please don't make the faucets run water. We like it this way."

"I want my root beer," wailed Petey. He looked ready to cry. We all felt pretty sad.

"There are a lot of milk bottles in the kitchen," said Mr. Pudgins. "Why don't you each fill two bottles with your favorite kind of drink and put them in the refrigerator. That should be enough for a long while."

It was pretty hard for me to decide on my favorite flavors. But not for Pete. He clumped right downstairs and got two quarts of root beer. Janey decided on one grape pop and one orange. I finally took a quart of limeade and one of grape pop. Gosh, that stuff was good! Then from the basement came an awful banging and clanging. The pipes rattled. They gurgled. Then it was quiet. I ran to the faucet in the kitchen and turned it on. Nothing but water. The bathtub faucet? Nothing but water. Only the washbowl seemed to run a little orange now and then.

Mr. Pudgins insisted that Petey and Jane have a bath and get the purple off of them. They didn't want to at first, but when they thought about it, they knew that Mom would be mad if she found they had been bathing in grape pop.

The house was all quiet when Mother and Dad came home. After Mr. Pudgins had left, I heard them in the kitchen. "My heavens, Jack, look at all the pop in the refrigerator. Bottles and bottles of the stuff."

"Good heavens!" came Dad's voice. "Where did it come from?"

"I suppose Johnny had a sale. I guess it can't hurt them," said Mother. I smiled to myself in the dark. Wouldn't they be surprised if they knew the truth, though? Then from the bathroom came Mother's voice again. "Jack, I've told you over and over to call that plumber. He's just got to check the rust in the pipes. The cold water is colored with orange."

I wanted to tell her it was really orange pop, but I was too sleepy. I decided to wait until morning. And in the morning I decided she wouldn't believe me. Sometimes after that the neighbors kidded Mother about letting her youngsters take a bath in grape pop, but she only laughed. She knew that they really hadn't.

6. Mr. Pudgins and the Flying Bathtub

I WAS fiddling with my radio and slowly getting un-
dressed for bed, but not very enthusiastically. It was a
hot August night as only an August night can be.
Mother and Dad had gone out for dinner at the
Smiths'. Dad had moaned about having to wear a coat
on such a night, but he had it on when he left. Mr.
Pudgins had discarded his to give Jane and Pete their
bath. From the bathroom I could hear splashing noises
and high squeals. That was Pete and Jane.

"John! Come here!"

That was Mr. Pudgins, and he sounded desperate.

I ran. There was Mr. Pudgins on his knees, hanging
on to the bathtub while Janey and Pete were playing
around in a tub full of bubble bath. Mr. Pudgins' nose
was quivering, and when that large a thing quivers,
everything seems to.

"Grab the tub," he ordered. "Must be some gas in that bubble bath. The bathtub's trying to float away."

Sure enough it was. It came loose from the wall with an awful rip, and I grabbed hold of the side and hung on. Petey and Jane clapped their hands and squealed. "Let go, Johnny. We want to go up." But I hung on. Only my feet were now off the floor.

"Hopeless," muttered Mr. Pudgins. "Might as well let her go. Climb in, Johnny."

"But my clothes?"

"They'll dry, lad. Do drop your shoes over."

I popped into the tub, and we floated out through the window and into the sky. I was in front near the faucets, Pete behind me, and then Janey. Sitting on the back edge of the tub smoking his pipe and very unconcerned was Mr. Pudgins. "Give the right faucet a twist, Johnny, or we'll sail out of town."

I did, and we gently turned right. It was wonderful —much better than a plane. And it was such a hot night that we didn't feel the least bit cold. Down below we could see the Johnsons' big police dog, and he barked like mad as we went over. Janey dropped a big glob of bubbly stuff on his nose, and he rubbed and rubbed it in the grass trying to get it off.

Mr. Hinkleberry was out hoeing his garden, and he opened his mouth so wide when he saw us floating in

the tub that I yearned to toss some bubbles in the hole. "Lovely evening, sir," said Mr. Pudgins. "Lovely."

Mr. Hinkleberry said nothing. He just gasped.

"A little to the left now, Johnny," said Mr. Pudgins.

I turned the hot-water faucet left and around we went. I just kept on turning, and we went round and round. "More, more!" yelled Petey. I began to feel dizzy.

"No. That is quite enough," said Mr. Pudgins. "Gently left, my lad." So I gently turned left.

Two sparrows came and sat on the edge of the tub, and Janey held out her soapy hand. Each of them pecked at the white stuff and then sat back and scolded her. It smelled of carnations, but I don't imagine it would taste good even to a bird. Right in front of us now was the Smiths' house, and I knew Mother and Dad must be sitting in the living room sweltering, when they might have been out sailing in a tub with us.

"Let's go lower and just float around the house," I said. "How do we do that?"

"I suppose you might pull the plug," said Mr. Pudgins. "Not too much now."

I pulled the plug, and sure enough, we went gradually down. Janey whispered, "Look, there's Mommy in the kitchen. Hello, Mommy." She almost fell out as she tried to knock on the window.

Mother looked up just as Mr. Pudgins' face went by the window glowing in the light of his pipe. She looked startled.

"Daddy, Daddy, Daddy!" shrieked Pete as we passed a living-room window. But Dad was talking to Mr. Smith and didn't hear. We could see Mother rushing in from the kitchen talking excitedly.

Then, as we drifted by the other side of the living room, Dad was saying, "You must have been sampling some of the drinks. Have you ever heard the like, Art?" That was Mr. Smith's name. They both laughed.

Mother turned away toward the window, and Janey waved enthusiastically at her, but I don't suppose Mother could see us. Instead she saw only Mr. Pudgins and his pipe as he sailed past, sitting on the end of the tub, his legs crossed, and leaning back to enjoy the summer evening. We couldn't stay longer, but we heard Mother say as we drifted down the street. "Look! Look! Didn't you see that?" But of course they hadn't.

I stuck the plug back in the hole, and we floated up near the treetops again. "There's Mike," yelled Pete. "Hi, Mike. See me, Mike. I'm floating."

Mike, who is four like Pete, stopped his bike and looked around and then looked some more for Pete. But he never thought of looking up, so he didn't see us.

On the corner of Main Street and Pearl we dipped a little lower, and Jimmy Sterrett, a reporter friend of Dad's, came driving along in his flivver. Pete shouted, "Hey, Jimmy! Jimmy! Jimmy!" and Janey joined right in. Jane's and Pete's shrieks were so loud that Jimmy did look up for just a second. Then, wham, he crashed into the car ahead!

As we floated up over a building, we heard Jimmy saying, "But, Officer, I tell you it was a bathtub."

"Bathtubs, is it?" came the officer's voice more softly as we drifted away. "Flying disks, flying platters, and now flying bathtubs. What won't you think of next?"

Mr. Pudgins smiled just a little, and so did I.

We were floating toward home when Petey saw some smoke coming from a chimney. "Look, a fire."

"Let's go see, please. I wanta see a chimney from up here," said Janey.

"All right, kiddies, just one look. Turn a little bit that way, Johnny."

So I did. "Why would anyone have a fire on a hot night like this?" I mused.

"An incinerator, I suppose, my boy." Mr. Pudgins stopped puffing on his pipe to twist and look ahead. "Not too close, now."

"What's a sinnerater? Something bad?" piped Pete.

"Oh, it burns up rubbish and cans and things like that, stupid," I said, looking back at him.

That did it. I wasn't watching closely enough, and we were stuck — right on top of that chimney. Whoof! Everyone got a mouthful of smoke, and then it stopped. I guess we had plugged up the hole.

"Now this is a predicament," muttered Mr. Pudgins. "But keep calm."

Janey hung way over the side. "Let's slide down the roof. I've always wanted to slide down the roof."

"I wanta fly." Pete began kicking his feet and throwing foam about. "Let's fly."

"Say, look down there," I shouted. "Lookit the smoke coming out of the house. Boy, a real fire."

"No, not exactly, John," said Mr. Pudgins, "but since the smoke can't come out of the chimney, it is going through the house. We had better get away from here. Let's rock the ship. Right . . . now left . . . now right."

"I'm getting awfully hot," said Janey because the water was heating up.

About then a man rushed out of the house, looked up at the chimney, and just stared. I suppose it was something of a surprise seeing the bathtub perched like a lollipop on the end of his chimney. We could hear sirens. "Get off of there! Do yah hear me?" The man acted mad, jumping up and down and shaking his fist. "Get off of there!" he yelled.

"That is just what we are endeavoring to do, my man," answered Mr. Pudgins calmly. "All right, children, rock. One two, one two, one two." The water sloshed and the tub began to wiggle. It scraped along the edge, and then we were off. The sirens sounded mighty close now. We drifted into a soft little cloud just as the engines screeched to a stop.

"All right, men. Hoses out." It was pretty exciting. We pushed part of the cloud aside and looked right down at the engines.

"It was a bathtub," shouted the man.

"Must be a smoke case. Too much smoke will do it, mister," said a fireman. "Get the doctor, Mac."

As we floated off, the man was screaming even more angrily, "But it *was* a bathtub." And then a little softer, "I think."

"Homeward, Johnny. Bedtime, I'm sure," directed Mr. Pudgins.

We were almost there when Janey whispered in surprise, "Johnny, the water. Lookit the water."

"Good heavens!" said Mr. Pudgins, "it's almost gone."

Just as he said that, we started down, down, down. "The plug, the plug!" I yelled. "Who's got the plug?"

"I dropped it," wailed Petey. "I dropped it right over the side when we were in that cloud."

"Get set to land," said Mr. Pudgins. "Easy does it, lads. Oh, not a tree."

But there we were perched in a big old maple tree about six feet off the ground.

"Where are we?" whispered Petey.

"I think it's the McCrackens', and they've got an awfully mean dog. How'll we ever get out?" I asked.

"You climb down and get the hose. Surely they'll have their hose around on such a night, and I'll pop out and find a stone to fit the drain," said Mr. Pudgins. He disappeared over the side and waved to us from below.

"Quiet, Petey. Not even a whisper, Janey. We don't want to get that dog started," I whispered, and I slid down the tree. It was a dandy for climbing. I scouted around, and sure enough, I found the hose in a corner of the yard. As quietly as I could, I pulled it toward the tree. Mr. Pudgins was already seated on the end of the tub. I could see his pipe glowing. I poked the hose up at him, then ran back to turn it on. It was going full blast when I heard the dog. Wow! Did I take off fast for the tree with the hound right behind me. One slip and he would have had fresh meat. Me. Luckily, my bare feet were good for a hold on the tree, and I made it up and into the tub. It was filling fast, and I could see Mr. Pudgins reach in his pocket, pull out a tiny envelope, and empty some powdery stuff in the water.

Slowly we started to float up. The hose pulled loose from the tub, and the full force of the water hit the dog right in the face. He yowled, and the back door of the house opened. Mr. McCracken came running out. As we turned toward home, we could hear Mr. Mc-Cracken shouting to his wife, "Maggie, Maggie, come see what some durn kid has done. Hung our hose in the maple tree."

We all laughed out loud. In fact, we were still laughing when we sailed in the window and settled down in the usual corner of the bathroom. Mr. Pudgins got to work and quickly had everyone snug in bed.

Later on I heard Mother and Dad come in, because they were arguing about Mother's behavior at the party.

"I did see a bathtub," she said crossly.

"Haaha . . . ohohoho," roared Dad. "Listen, you must have been in that state where some people see pink elephants. But a bathtub . . . ha ho ho."

"I'll have you know," said Mother, "that I had only tomato juice."

"Maybe it was the heat," said Dad, "but it sure was a funny idea of yours."

He started to laugh again, and I heard Mother say "Hush." Then I drifted back to sleep.

7. Mr. Pudgins and the Train

WE WERE IN QUARANTINE. Believe me, those are dismal words to hear. It was Janey who had scarlet fever, but the rest of us had to stay at home even so. Only Mr. Pudgins was unafraid of the big red sign that said "Keep Out." He had had scarlet fever, so every Saturday he came in to give Mother a chance to get out. And we were glad to see him. By the second Saturday, Janey was feeling well enough to be up and about, and that day Mr. Pudgins brought his little train over for us to play with. I opened the box and was a little disappointed. It wasn't an electric train.

"Gosh! This is a baby train," I said. "A windup."

"On the contrary. This is one of my own inventions. It runs by a power pill. That does away with electricity and its dangers. Now let's set it up."

"Oh, my. What a lot of tracks," said Janey.

"And switches, too, said Petey. "Oh, my."

Jane laid track out into the kitchen, and we could hear her clattering around. "Hey, where you putting that track, Janey?" I yelled.

"Just underneath the refrigerator and kitchen table," she answered.

"Sounds as if you're moving pans," I shouted back.

"I am. I'm trying to get the track to go up into the pan cupboard and down again," she answered.

"Boy, this will be fun," I said to Mr. Pudgins as I laid track underneath the davenport, under the big armchair he liked to sit in, out again and around to form a figure eight, and then down the hall.

"Come on and see what I've done," said Petey.

I stopped and ran into his bedroom. He had run the track under his bed twice and then into the closet, where he had made a hill up onto a shelf and down again. "Say, that's good, Pete," I said. "Now be sure the track is put together tightly. And then come help join up with Jane's track and mine."

It took us a long time to get the track all together, and when it was all set, Mr. Pudgins set the train on the track in the living room. All three of us lay down on our tummies to watch — Jane's blond pigtails next to Pete's shiny blond head right next to my straight blond stuff. The train was a freight. It had a bright-red engine and coal car, a yellow refrigerator car, a black tanker, a green flat car, and a red caboose.

"Isn't it pretty?" asked Janey.

"Let's get it started," said Pete as he bounced. "Start it."

Mr. Pudgins took out a yellow pill and dropped it in the cab of the engine. Then he took out a black pill and put that in the sand dome.

"What's that for?" asked Petey.

"That is for smoke," said Mr. Pudgins. "My own invention."

"And what's the yellow one for?" asked Janey.

"The yellow pill is the power. Also my invention."

"How do you get it started?" I asked.

"I take a little coal from my pipe, put it on the pill, shut the cab, and wait."

"Will it take long?" asked Petey, watching the train impatiently.

"Not too long, I trust," said Mr. Pudgins.

Whhhooom! That was the train starting, and it started fast. From just sitting in front of our noses, it was suddenly zipping under the davenport, under the chair, and around and around the figure eight.

"Throw the switch," yelled Janey.

I threw the switch, and then we ran after the train to the kitchen. It puffed under the refrigerator and under the table, then climbed towards the pan cupboard.

"Lookit, lookit," said Petey, "it's going to hit the pans." And it did.

Crash bang! Mr. Pudgins came running. "Any damage?"

"This pan is all right," said Janey.

"So is this cake tin," said Petey.

"The pans are all okay, but is the train all right?" I asked.

Mr. Pudgins looked at the engine very closely and then put it back on the track. "Everything is all set, but you'd better change that curve, Janey. It's too sharp."

We left Janey fixing her curve and followed the train into the bedroom. It would disappear under the bed once, then under the bed again. Whoosh! It was gone in the closet. Every now and then it whistled. And then suddenly it appeared to run under the beds again. Petey wanted to let it run and run in this room, but I insisted we try the kitchen again.

"Are you ready, Jane?"

"All set. Come ahead," Janey called back.

So we threw the switch, and the little train chugged down the hall and into the kitchen. This time there was no accident. We kept running from room to room and having a wonderful time chasing the train. By now it was carrying some small Lincoln logs, a load of beads, and a few assorted Tinker Toys. Suddenly Mr. Pudgins remarked, "Children, does it seem to you to be getting dark?"

We looked up. Something was wrong. A heavy dark cloud seemed to be lying next to the ceiling and slowly settling.

"Bouncing butterballs!" said Mr. Pudgins. He always said that when he really was surprised.

"Is something wrong?" asked Janey.

"When you had that accident . . ." said Mr. Pudgins.

"Oh, my!" said Petey.

"Yes, we must have knocked the smoke pill back with the fuel pill, and it's burning up too fast. Not that this is like real smoke, but it's getting dark."

"I can't see very well," I said.

"Catch the train," ordered Mr. Pudgins.

"There it goes," said Janey. "I . . . I think." The smoke was really down upon us now.

"I don't see it," said Petey.

"Neither do I," said I.

"Now don't get excited," said Mr. Pudgins.

"It's getting awfully thick," wailed Petey. "Where are you, Janey?"

It really was getting thick. I couldn't see my hand when I held it out straight before me. "Johnny," said Mr. Pudgins' voice in the smoke.

"Here I am, Mr. Pudgins," I answered.

"Johnny, grab Janey's hand; and Jane, you find Pete. Now if I can just find Johnny."

I stumbled around and bumped my head on the floor lamp, then whammed against the end table. I was more cautious after that. Finally, I bumped into Jane. She had corraled Pete. We stumbled around some more, and suddenly out of the dark came a hand that grabbed my collar. It was Mr. Pudgins'. All during this time we would hear a faint whistle now and then. Once something shot out of the dark and right past me. I jumped. Petey yelled, "There she goes." But we were too late. It was gone.

"Now," said Mr. Pudgins, "we must have a plan."

"Oh my," said Janey, "it's awfully dark."

"I hear it," yelled Petey. He seemed to think that the dark made us slightly deaf.

"I think," said Mr. Pudgins, "that we must first find the tracks."

"We'd better crawl," I suggested. "Otherwise we might step right over them."

"I need my hands to crawl," said Jane. "And my hands are holding somebody else's hands."

"Keep hold of hands, but wiggle forward," commanded Mr. Pudgins. So we wiggled. How I wished I could have seen him wiggling, too. And then simultaneously we hit the track.

"I feel it," said Janey. "I feel the track."

"Me too," yelled Petey. Far away we heard the whistle of the train.

"Grab it when it goes by," I ordered.

We relaxed for a moment. And then whoooommm! There was the train. Pete grabbed. Jane grabbed. I grabbed. Mr. Pudgins grabbed. And we all missed.

"Dear me," said Mr. Pudgins. "This won't do at all."

We heard the train rushing around the figure eight. Then wham!

"I guess that did it," came Jane in a proud voice. "I put my foot on the track.

"I've got it. I've got it!" yelled Petey.

"Crawl toward us, Pete," said Mr. Pudgins. "And for heaven's sake, don't miss us."

"The wheels are still going," said Petey, and then he bumped right into me. Mr. Pudgins reached out of the dark and took the engine. Then he started toward the door. We could hear him bumping around. "Ouch!" he said. "Wow," he muttered. "Oweee," he groaned. He was having a hard time. "Made it," he called, and we all felt a burst of fresh air.

"I'm emptying out the pill," said Mr. Pudgins. "And now for the back door. Can you open that, Johnny?"

So I started toward the kitchen. Right off I ran into Janey and Pete.

"Look out," said Janey crossly.

"I am," I answered. "Only it doesn't help. Ouch!" I hit the corner of the kitchen door. Well, at least I had gotten that far. I felt my way into the kitchen and then remembered the fan Mother had there to drive out smoke and odors, so I snapped that on. It started up with a rush of sound, and I could feel the smoke whirling around. Finally I got to the door, found the knob, and pulled it open. Boy, that sunny outdoors looked wonderful! I had to blink at so much light. Then I swung the door back and forth to suck out the smoke. I could see into the kitchen a little bit now. Mr. Pudgins had opened some windows in the bedrooms, and the smoke was billowing out. Things had just about cleared out when we heard the siren.

"A fire," yelled Petey. "A fire. Can we go?"

"I should say not," said Mr. Pudgins. "You're in quarantine."

"Gee whillikers," I said, "it's coming closer and closer. Wouldn't you know I'd miss a fire right in the neighborhood?"

The three of us pressed our noses against the window pane. "There it comes," said Janey. And sure enough, it was a big hook-and-ladder truck swinging right down our street.

"Lookit all the people out there," said Pete.

There were a lot of people all gathered on our front sidewalk.

"Hey," I said in surprise, "it's us. They think we're on fire."

"Bouncing butterballs," said Mr. Pudgins sinking down in the armchair. "Well, let's keep calm." He took out his pipe again and was just drawing hard on it when a fireman burst in the door. It was open, of course, to let the smoke out.

"Where's the fire? Where's the fire, bub?" said the fireman. Another and another and still another came in the door. They had their axes ready, and out on the truck they were starting to unwind the hose. One of the firemen carried a chemical fire extinguisher. It was pretty impressive.

Mr. Pudgins looked up from lighting his pipe with a surprised expression. "Fire?" he said. "There's no fire here."

"Listen," said the first fireman, "we got four calls from neighbors, and they said the smoke was pouring out of the door and windows. Where there's smoke, there's fire."

"Well, not in this case," said Mr. Pudgins.

I snickered.

"Oh yeah!" said the fireman. "If it wasn't a fire, what was it then?"

Mr. Pudgins rose from the chair and smiled at the fireman. "Nothing to be alarmed at, gentlemen. Just a little invention of mine."

"Some invention," growled the fireman. "We ought to haul you in for a false alarm. We'll just take a look around anyway."

"I'm in quarantine," Janey spoke up proudly, "for SCARLET FEVER."

"Good gosh! What next?" said the firemen in disgust. I noticed they were careful to stay away from us. They tramped all through the house, but they couldn't find a thing. We could hear them muttering as they left.

We had had a wonderful afternoon. Petey stood at Mr. Pudgins' chair.

"What'll we do now?" he asked plaintively.

"Why pick up the track, of course," said Mr. Pudgins. "Then supper and to bed." And that's exactly what we did.

8. Mr. Pudgins' Circus

THIS WAS THE LAST SATURDAY we were to be in quarantine for scarlet fever, and the circus was in town. Of course we were going to miss it, so we felt pretty sad.

"Why is everyone so glum, Johnny?" asked Mr. Pudgins.

"It's the circus," I grumped from a corner.

"I wanta go," wailed Petey, and he started to cry.

"I want to go too," moaned Janey, and she started to cry.

"Oh, hush up, Janey," I growled. "It's all your fault. You didn't have to go and get scarlet fever."

It looked as if we were going to get into a good fight. And I felt just like having one. Then Mr. Pudgins said, "Let's have our own circus."

"Goody! Goody!" yelled Jane and Pete. They stopped crying immediately.

"Nuts!" I said crossly. "That's baby stuff."

"All right, Johnny. You stay in here and feel sorry for yourself," said Mr. Pudgins. "Come, Pete and Jane, let's go outside."

I was afraid I might really miss some fun, so I followed after them. Mr. Pudgins put some boxes on the grass.

"Those are seats," he said.

"Who's going to sit there?" I growled.

"Why we are, of course," said Mr. Pudgins.

Then who is going to perform?" I asked just as nastily as I could. I certainly felt horrible.

"My friends," said Mr. Pudgins. He didn't pay any attention to my nastiness, and I began to feel better.

"All right," I said. "I'll help."

"Then go and get some bags. Now Pete, you and Jane can blow up the balloons. Take them out to the car and let Podo do the blowing. They will float then."

We all ran to do our jobs. It took me quite a while to find paper bags, and when I looked out the window I could see that Peter was holding a big bunch of balloons while Jane kept leaning into the trunk of the car. Suddenly Pete started to float right up into the air. Janey turned around, saw him, and grabbed his feet. I rushed out to help her.

"Go away," she said. "This is fun pushing Pete through the air."

"My, my," said Mr. Pudgins as we rounded the corner of the house. "What is our balloon man doing?"

"I'm floating," said Petey happily. "I'm floating."

"Tie him to the clothespole, Janey, so he won't get away. If he wants to see the circus from up there, I've no objection."

Petey hung on the clothes pole for almost five minutes and then he said, "I want to get down, Mr. Pudgins."

So Janey untied him, and together they fastened the balloons to the lilac bush.

"Here are the paper bags, Mr. Pudgins," I said.

"Oh yes," he said vaguely. "Just fill them with

peanuts and popcorn. It wouldn't be a circus without peanuts and popcorn."

"Oh yes, peanuts and popcorn. But where are they?"

"Over there," he said waving toward the garden. "Hunt for them."

Janey and Pete came along to help me. They love to eat. We crawled everywhere, looking, and it was slightly hard on mother's flowers. Suddenly Pete yelled, "I found it! I found it!"

Janey and I rushed over. He was digging in the ground at a few pieces of popcorn, and suddenly up burst a geyser of popcorn. It gushed high into the air and fell down on us like snow. Janey held out her skirt, I pulled off my shirt, and Pete ran around holding paper sacks in the air. We filled everything in a hurry, and it started to pile up.

"How do you shut it off?" I called to Mr. Pudgins who was relaxing in a lawn chair.

"Try saying 'Stop,'" he suggested.

All three of us yelled "STOP!" And sure enough, the next bursts were lower and lower and lower, until it stopped.

"Now where are the peanuts?" I muttered.

"We haven't tried the rock garden," said Janey.

We hurried over there and on the rocks, in between rocks, under rocks were peanuts in the shell. Hundreds and thousands and millions of peanuts. It took Pete's big wagon and Dad's wheelbarrow to get them all back to Mr. Pudgins.

"Whew! That was some job," I said, wiping my fore-head.

"Let's have the circus," said Pete, grabbing a handful of peanuts and munching.

"Sit down," said Mr. Pudgins. "The show is about to begin."

We were sitting facing our swings and trapeze bar. There was a toot of a horn, and then from the garage came a lot of little field mice carrying pint jars. They placed them in a circle. When they had finished that, the mice took zinnia stalks in their teeth and out from the garage drove ten little kittens — some tiger-striped, some yellow, and a few all black. The kittens jumped up on the fruit jars and snarled. Now from the garage ran a big field mouse with a tiny whip in his mouth. He put those cats through all sorts of tricks. They sat up on their haunches; they jumped through a dandelion hoop; they danced on their hind legs; they leaped across six jars set side by side. It was a wonderful act. You should have heard us applaud when it finished.

"Hey, give me some popcorn," whispered Janey. I was most willing to oblige. I handed her a whole shovelful.

The next act was bunnies on the flying trapeze. They swung by their ears, and you should have seen those bunnies twirl, whirl, and catch each other. Just as they started back for the garage at the end of their perform-ance, we saw Podo, the dodo bird, coming toward

them. And you know what he was? A clown, of course. He was wearing Janey's doll's bonnet and lots and lots of clothes. He was waving so hard at us that he bumped right into the littlest rabbit, and was that rabbit mad! He wanted to fight right away. Podo was very willing to fight, but first he started to take off his jackets. Podo threw the rabbit a green jacket. Then he

took off a patched red one. The rabbit was struggling to put up his paws to fight, but he was getting slowly buried. Next he caught a blue and yellow plaid jacket. Now a pink organdy blouse.

The rabbit was gasping. And still the clothes came. A white shirt, a pair of baggy pants, a pair of yellow patched overalls, a white T shirt. The rabbit was staggering. Podo threw a long flannel nightie at the rabbit, and he fell over backward with all the clothes on top

of him. Podo paraded around proudly in a suit of long
underwear and clasped his hands together, shouting,
"The winnah!" Suddenly he looked down and saw his
underwear for the first time. He let out a little embar-
rassed shriek and fled from the ring. We all sat back
and laughed. Podo was a wonderful clown.

"Gosh, this is fun!" I said.

"More peanuts," said Pete.

Jip, the McCracken's dog, walked in on his hind legs, and he looked mean — just as mean as he had the night we landed in his backyard in a bathtub. He carried a whip in his paw and cracked it loudly. It made us all jump. Behind him ran four skunks, and they formed a circle. Jip soon had them performing like a machine. When he barked once, they would run round and round the circle, single file like Arabian horses. Two quick barks, and they would reverse and double up. It was remarkable.

But then Jip did it. He cracked the last skunk with the whip, and it made a dull thud when the thong landed. We jumped. The skunk just turned his back on him and very slowly raised his tail. We knew what was coming now.

"Run, run!" I shrieked. And you should have seen us scoot. Even Mr. Pudgins bounced right along with us. We heard an awful yelp from Jip and knew the skunk had hit. All of us giggled. And then Jip, in his frantic effort to escape, ran headlong into the lilac bush. Of

course he got caught in the balloon strings. How he tugged and struggled to get loose, and finally the whole bunch of balloons broke away from the bush and started to float off. Jip floated right with them. We just howled.

Mrs. McCracken told Mother the next Saturday that Jip disappeared for a whole week and came limping home smelling of skunk. She just couldn't understand it. But we could. Those Podo-blown balloons must really have floated. And Jip evidently had time to do some doggy thinking, for he's a pleasanter dog now.

9. Mr. Pudgins and Annabelle

Annabelle was Mr. Pudgins' car. And what a car it was —an old Model-T coupe. You know what those look like. It was a cracker box on wheels. Whenever Mr. Pudgins drove up in her, we would beg for a ride. And he always said, "No!" — until this particular September day. Mother was going downtown for lunch and some shopping, so Mr. Pudgins suggested he take us on a picnic. Mother said "No" at first because Annabelle was so very old. But at last she relented.

Gollee! Were we relieved and excited! Janey made peanut-butter sandwiches, I put chocolate milk in the thermos, and Pete found some cookies and bananas. Then we raced for the car. We looked for Podo when we opened the trunk to put the lunch in, but he wasn't there.

97

"I have to leave him home sometimes," said Mr. Pudgins, guessing our thoughts. "He can be a nuisance. Now hop in the car."

We had to squeeze a little to get the three of us and Mr. Pudgins on that small seat. But we made it.

"This is fun, up so high," said Janey. "I can see everything."

"Annabelle is a lady, and real ladies keep their skirts off the ground," said Mr. Pudgins. He struggled with the starter. Nothing happened. Out he climbed with a crank in his hand. "Kick the throttle in when she grabs, Johnny." He spun the crank and he spun the crank and he spun the crank some more. At last whirrah, whirrah, jickety jounce. The motor started. We bounced sideways. We jiggled and jaggled.

"She'ssss got lotsssof act . . . ttion," I sputtered. It was pretty hard to talk because the words kept getting jumbled up on the way out of you.

"Of course, Annabellllle has zzzzipp," said Mr. Pudgins, jouncing too. "It willllllbe betterrr on the highway."

As we were putting along a country road, Mr. Pudgins turned to me and said, "Would you like to steer for a while, Johnny?"

"Oh jeepers, can I? Can I? Let me at it."

"Now take it easy, my boy." Mr. Pudgins leaned forward and screwed a little switch. Then he simply handed me the steering wheel.

"Look! Look!" screamed Janey excitedly. "It comes off."

"Just remote control. One of my own inventions," said Mr. Pudgins modestly. He put his head down under the dashboard to listen to the motor. "Sounds pretty good for such an old lady, eh?" He acted very pleased.

I tried turning the wheel left, and the thing really worked. I thought he might have been fooling me. We were driving very slowly now. Mr. Pudgins seemed to be looking for something. About this time we sighted a farmer hoeing his corn. Whirrah, whirrah, jickety jounce. Slowly we approached. "I say," said Mr. Pudgins, leaning out the window and using both hands as a megaphone. "Where is Donnavan's stream?"

"You durn fool," shouted the farmer, "put your hands on the wheel!" He couldn't see that I was steer-

ing, so we were past him before we found out about the stream. Pete had a turn at steering and so did Janey. It was wonderful to have a wheel that could be passed back and forth. Mr. Pudgins just leaned back in his corner and smoked.

Finally Mr. Pudgins took the wheel back and turned into a little meadow with a stream. We followed along until we came to the lake, and with a snort and puff Annabelle stopped. We piled out of the car, spread a blanket, and sat down to eat. Boy! That lunch tasted wonderful.

"Wish we had a boat," murmured Pete as he finished his cookie.

"Oh, me too," said Jane, chewing on her banana.

"Looks like a good lake for fish," I commented.

"By all means, let us go fishing," said Mr. Pudgins. We looked at him a little surprised. "Johnny, you climb on the trunk, and Jane and Pete can sit on the hood."

"You mean of Annabelle?" I gasped.

"And why not?" He walked over to the car, opened the hood, and we heard an awful clinking clanking noise. "All right, children. Come."

We did. He tied a rope around Pete and Jane and ran the rope through the window, where he tied it to the wheel. I hopped on the trunk, which jutted out pretty

straight, and he handed me a fishing line. "All set?" We nodded. Whirrah, whirrah, jickety jounce went Annabelle. Mr. Pudgins hopped in the car and started driving right towards the water.

"Oh, oh! We'll get drownded," whimpered Pete.

Then salop, salop we were in the lake. No, we were *on* the lake. Annabelle was floating. She really made a wonderful boat. Pete and Jane dipped their feet in the water and giggled when the minnows tickled them. And I caught fish. Yes, sir! I caught three good-sized bass. I was proud as punch. Suddenly we all realized it was getting pretty late, and Mr. Pudgins gave Annabelle the gun as he headed for shore. He swerved to miss a log, and then it happened. The rope jammed the steering wheel, and we started whirling around and around like a saucer in the fun house. I stuck my hand through the back window to hold on, but the rest of me flew straight out in the air. I could see Jane and Pete flying around, too.

"I'm an airplane," yelled Pete.

"I'm a stork," shrieked Jane. That was a funny bird to pick.

"I'm Superman!" I shouted. "Let her rip." I could see Mr. Pudgins tinkering with the steering wheel, and finally he jerked the rope loose. He tossed the steering wheel to me. "Take her in, please, Johnny. I'm exhausted."

And, boy, I did! We were all a little dizzy, so Annabelle just weaved up to the shore. That flying had dried us off, so we started right out for home. When we turned back on the highway, Mr. Pudgins opened An-

nabelle up, and then we really jiggled. "I . . . I
. . . thinknnkkkk, I'I'I'mmmmmlossssing a tooothh,"
said Janey.

And she was. The jiggling was shaking it loose. Pete
and I were so interested in watching Jane's tooth that
we didn't see the big coal truck ahead of us that was
slowly moving up a long hill. "Hold on!" shouted Mr.
Pudgins. "We're going to jump it."

We looked up in surprise, and ooooof, my stomach seemed to fall! Annabelle gave a big push with her rear wheels, and there we were in the air. Only she didn't push quite hard enough. Plop! We came down on top of the coal, and the motor stopped. Mr. Pudgins couldn't get it to turn over again.

"Now what?" I asked. People were staring at us as they whizzed by the truck. And we must have looked a little peculiar. Annabelle, though, was still the prim lady, and I knew she must be disgusted at getting her wheels so dirty. "Shall I climb over and signal the man to stop?"

"Capital idea, Johnny. All that whirling in the water must have knocked something loose. Here, tie this rope on just to be safe."

It was pretty exciting to step out of the door way up in the air like that, and the truck was really whipping along now. I had to just inch my way past Annabelle's hood, and then I crawled on my hands and knees over the coal to the truck's cab. With the wind biting my face, I lay down on my stomach and leaned over the windshield. The man inside was watching the road with a bored expression. I tapped gently on the window. I didn't want to frighten him. He looked up, and then how we swerved! I was scared Annabelle might be thrown right off. The truck pulled to the side of the road and stopped with a jerk.

"You darn fool kid. Whatcha doin' up there?" shouted the driver as he jumped from the cab.

I just grinned.

"Get down in a hurry, yah hear me?" I started moving back over the coal, and then. . . .

"Excuse me, sir," came Mr. Pudgins' quiet voice.

The driver looked up and saw Mr. Pudgins leaning out of Annabelle, who was perched a little screwily on the coal. His mouth dropped so low I could see his tonsils vibrating.

"We are in a predicament, as you can see," said Mr. Pudgins. "Johnny just wanted you to stop so that we can get off of here."

"Thunderation," gasped the driver. He was pretty upset: "I've picked up lots of things in a load, but never a car."

Mr. Pudgins had climbed out over the coal, and I got back in while he cranked. Whirrah, whirrah, jickety jounce. Annabelle was singing her happy work song again. Mr. Pudgins tipped his hat to the man, worked his way back to the door, and climbed in. For a moment we just bounced, and then with an awful racket we started forward, ground over the top of the cab, and sailed through the air to land in front of the truck. We didn't stop to talk to the driver. We were much too late. But we all waved good-bye as he stood with his mouth open, scratching his head.

"Let's jump again," said Pete.

"That's fun," said Jane.

"No, something is out of kilter with Annabelle's jumping equipment. We'll try another day," Mr. Pudgins objected.

Much too quickly we jounced our way home and stopped in front of our house. Mother ran out, and I could tell she was a little worried. It was getting pretty late. "Why, Johnny, where did you get so dirty?"

"Oh, just on some coal. But look at my fish." And I dragged out my fish to show her.

"Mother, we had the most peachy time," said Janey.

"Perfectly perfect," added Pete.

We did want to tell Mother all about our day. But you can't ever really describe such a perfect time. We gave up trying. Still, at night when the crickets were singing, we kept talking of Mr. Pudgins and the wonderful Annabelle.

10. The Mirror Children Again

"GOOD-BYE, GOOD-BYE!" we all three shouted to Mother and Dad as they climbed into the car. This was Homecoming, and they were pretty excited about going back to the university and seeing their old friends. Since Mr. Pudgins had come to stay with us, I didn't mind too much not being able to go along.

For an hour or so everything went smoothly. Pete and Jane played Mommy and Daddy, and I listened to the football game on the radio. Then from the bedroom came Jane's voice. It certainly sounded cross.

"I want someone to play with," said Janey.

"I'm here," said Petey. "You can play with me."

"Oh you," said Janey in disgust. "I can play with you any old time." They were in their bedroom, but we could hear them way out in the living room. Mr.

Pudgins was sitting in his armchair, and now he took out his pipe. I felt a thrill go through me. Something would really happen now.

"Come here, children," he called.

Jane and Pete came running. "Why don't you ask your little friends in the mirror to come and play?" asked Mr. Pudgins.

"Oh, goody, goody!" yelled Pete.

"Goody, goody!" screamed Janey.

"But no popcorn," said Mr. Pudgins.

I decided I'd like to have a look at Mirjohnny again, too, so all three of us went to the big mirror in the hall. We couldn't always get the mirror children out, because we had tried. But maybe now we could since Mr. Pudgins was here again and smoking away at his pipe. Each of us reached toward that other child. "Come on," I said.

"Please, come," said Janey. And the two of us pulled. Out stepped Mirjohnny and Mirjaney. But Mirpete just stood and looked at us.

"Give him a yank, Pete," I said.

"But, Johnny, I don't think I want to."

"Oh, go on," I said.

So Pete pulled Mirpete out, and there the six of us were. "Now what will we do?" asked Janey.

"Let's think," I suggested.

"We can play paper dolls," said Jane.

"No!" shouted the four boys.

"Football?" asked Pete.

"Hole in the ball," I answered.

"How about Old Maid?" suggested Mirjohnny.

"Say, that's a good idea. It's a lot of fun with so many."

Janey ran for the cards, and we all sat in a circle while she dealt them. We laughed and squealed. Petey didn't understand that he wasn't supposed to get the Old Maid, so he yelled for joy each time he got it. We played and laughed and played some more.

"Now let's go outside," said Mirjaney.

"I have to go to the bathroom," said Pete.

"Well, go on," I said. "We'll wait for you."

He'd been gone only a few minutes, and then we heard a funny noise from the hall. "Johnny . . . Johnny." Pete sounded worried so I ran. He was standing in front of the mirror with a very troubled expression on his face.

"I'm not there," he said and pointed at the mirror.

"Oh, sure you are," I said. Then I looked, and sure enough he wasn't reflected and neither was I. It gave me a funny feeling to look and not see myself.

"Gosh, this is bad. You know those are our reflections out there in the living room. Boy, we'd better not lose track of them."

"Hurry up," said Janey crossly, coming out of the living room to get us. "Now what's the matter?"

"Look in the mirror and see," said I.

Janey looked and then said excitedly, "Why, I don't see anything."

"That's right," I answered, "so don't lose Mirjaney. Let's go."

We got a surprise when we got back to the living room, for the mirror children were gone. My heart sank a little bit. "Hey, kids," we shouted. And then we heard some giggles. There they were, hiding on top of the draperies.

"Let's play hide and seek," said Mirjaney.

"Oh, no," said Jane, and I knew she had the same thought I did. They might be too good at the hiding.

"How about tag?" asked Mirjohnny.

That sounded better, so we trooped outside and started playing wood tag. "Say," I called after a while, "you're not playing fair. You keep floating up into the trees. We can't get you there."

"That's what I thought," said Mirjohnny and laughed.

It was a strenuous game. Not only did we have to run after the mirror children when we were "it," but we had to climb trees, jump in the air, and swing from branches.

"Let's stop," said Pete.

"I'm tired," said Jane.

"We aren't," said the three mirror children. They were sitting on the branches of the apple tree.

"Let's go see the world," said Mirjaney.

"Goody, goody!" said Mirpete.

"Oh no you can't!" we screamed.

"Just watch us and see," said Mirjohnny, and they started to float away.

"Mr. Pudgins! Mr. Pudgins!" yelled the three of us.

He came strolling to the door. "My goodness. What now?"

"Look! Look!" yelled Petey.

"They're flying away," called Janey.

"We must catch them," I moaned.

"Bouncing butterballs!" said Mr. Pudgins excitedly. "This calls for action. Go get Podo."

"You mean the dodo bird?" I asked.

"Of course." He handed me the key. I ran and opened the trunk, and there was Podo sitting in a corner, sleeping.

"Hey, Podo. Glubily," I yelled. I didn't know what it meant, but it seemed to wake him up. I grabbed him in my arms and ran back to Mr. Pudgins.

"Now, Podo," said Mr. Pudgins, "we want you to catch those children floating away over there." He waved his hand toward the sky where the mirror children were getting smaller and smaller.

"No!" said Podo.

"Don't be that way," said Mr. Pudgins crossly. "Just blow up a wind and go catch them."

"No!" said Podo.

"Oh, dear," said Janey. "I do so want to be able to see myself."

"Me too," wailed Petey.

"Look, Podo," I said, thinking fast. "I'll give you my new ring that lights in the dark and can write under water."

"Noooo," said Podo hesitatingly.

"I'll give you my big doll's new bonnet," said Jane.

"Welll," said Podo.

"I'll give you my rubber ball," said Pete.

"All right," said Podo. "I'll do it." By now the children had disappeared. "But won't I just blow them farther away with my wind?"

"Bouncing butterballs," said Mr. Pudgins. "He's right. I will just have to go along. Where's the clothes-line?"

Jane ran and got it from the garage, and when she came back, Mr. Pudgins was sitting on Podo's back, pipe in his mouth and cap set back on his head. With the rope, he made a loop and then twirled it over his head.

"He's a cowboy," said Pete.

"An air cowboy," said Jane.

"All right, Podo," said Mr. Pudgins. "Let's go."

We heard Podo suck in the air, and then whooooooo. . . . Janey grabbed the cherry tree, Pete fell flat on the ground, and I went over and over until I banged into the garage. When I got up, I could see Mr. Pudgins riding along on Podo and twirling the rope. For a moment he disappeared, and then whoooo, the

wind hit us in the face. We all rolled over on the grass. "Lie flat," I shouted. "They must be coming back."

"There's Mirjaney," yelled Jane.

And sure enough, floating over our heads was Mirjaney. Mirpete and Mirjohnny were right behind her. We saw Mr. Pudgins coming up quickly, and suddenly the loop shot out. It went over Mirjaney's head and down on her shoulders. Then Mr. Pudgins pulled the loop tight. They flew right over the house, and we rushed around in front to see what was happening. Mr. Pudgins had untied Mirjaney and hung her in the dodo's mouth. Now he twirled the rope over his head again and out it shot. This time Mirpete was caught. Mr. Pudgins tied him to the dodo's fluff of tail. They were certainly a sight — the little dodo with plump Mr. Pudgins astride of him and a child hanging at each end.

"Hey," I called. "Don't lose my reflection. There he goes!"

Mr. Pudgins nodded his head, and then they all blew along and into the cloud where Mirjohnny had just disappeared. Bits of the cloud started to break off and float away. They must be having an awful fight. Then we heard a shriek, and out came Mr. Pudgins smiling broadly as he puffed on his pipe, and Mirjohnny was floating way behind but securely tied with the rope.

They landed in the back yard, and Mr. Pudgins handed me the rope with Mirjohnny at the end. Jane grabbed Mirjaney's hand and started pulling her toward the front door, and Pete pulled Mirpete by the rope around his tummy. Into the house we went and marched back to the mirror. And then we shoved those children right in even though they didn't want to go.

"I'll never, never take her out again," said Janey. "I want to be able to see myself." And she made an awful face at the mirror. Mirjaney made the same horrible face right back at her.

"Look, I'm there again," said Pete. He smiled at the mirror, and Mirpete smiled back at him.

"I'm glad I've got my reflection back. Thanks loads, Mr. Pudgins," I said. "Gosh, that was scary!"

'And now, children," said Mr. Pudgins, "you promised the dodo bird some things."

"Oh, so we did," I said. I got my ring, Pete got his ball, and Jane the bonnet. Then we took them out to the dodo bird, who was sitting in the trunk waiting. Jane tied the bonnet around his head, and we had to struggle not to laugh. I slipped the ring on his claw, and it glowed in the dark. Pete shoved the ball in the other claw. As we shut the trunk, we could see Podo bouncing the ball by the light of his ring. And every now and then he reached a tiny wing toward his new bonnet, to feel if it were really there. He was singing, too:

> Whenever I strumbily in the sky
> And on my didily fiddily fly,
> I sing out with whiddily fiddily pie
> And grubily, dudsy is my cry.

We all hustled into the house, and the three of us went back to be sure that the mirror children were really there. They were. And never again did we take them out to play. It was too dangerous.

When Mother and Dad got home near suppertime, Janey rushed right out and told them all about the mirror children.

"Isn't it wonderful, Jack, how Mr. Pudgins is stimulating the children's imaginations?"

Dad gulped and said, "Oh, is that what it is?"

Mr. Pudgins just knocked the ashes from his pipe, smiled at us all with a very special twinkle in his eye, and departed with a bang and whir in Annabelle.

I said nothing. It was a good idea to have Mother think it was imagination.

11. Mr. Pudgins' Birthday Party

WE SAW MR. PUDGINS drive up with a whang and bang in Annabelle, but he took such a very long time getting into the house that we were all puzzled.

"Really, Jack," said Mother, "if he doesn't hurry, we are going to be late for the Hillenwhoops' dinner. And she's so fussy. Oh, dear!" Mother pushed at the black witch's hat on her head. "I could scream at this crazy hat. It's going to be screwgey all the time."

"Well, if you think I like going as the devil, you've another thought coming," exploded Dad, tugging at his tail which Pete was standing on. "Any grown woman who gives a fancy-dress Halloween party can expect folks to be late. I hate the whole idea."

"Daddy is a devil. Daddy is a devil," chanted Janey from her perch in the window. She was still looking for Mr. Pudgins.

"If you don't stop that, young lady, you'll see what kind of a devil I am."

"Are you a good witch, Mommy, like the nice ones in the *Wizard of Oz*?" asked Pete.

"Why, yes, I'm a nice witch. Oh, Jack . . ." Mother started to giggle. "Whoever thought we'd admit to the children that I'm a witch and you're a devil?"

Dad grinned just a little, then grabbed his pitchfork, and started to the door. "Come on, Witchy," he said. And just that moment the door swung open and there was Mr. Pudgins. We could hardly see him for the armload of packages. "My goodness!" he gasped, looking at Mother and Dad in their costumes.

"Some getup, eh?" grinned Dad. "Well, we're off. Looks as if you're set for something yourself."

"My birthday," explained Mr. Pudgins, dumping the packages in the kitchen. "I brought along a few things to celebrate."

"Have fun," called Mother and Dad. The door slammed shut behind them.

"Now, children," said Mr. Pudgins, "the first thing to do is set the table."

"Janey and I can do that," I said. And we did.

"Now," said Mr. Pudgins, "shall we play a game?"

"Yes, yes," yelled Petey.

"Let's pin a tail on the donkey. You always do that at birthday parties," said Janey.

"How fortunate," said Mr. Pudgins. "I just happen to have a donkey game and some tails here." He hung the donkey on the wall, then put a blindfold on Petey and whirled him around. At first, Petey started off in the opposite direction. It looked as if he might pin a tail on the davenport. But Mr. Pudgins gave him a shove in the right direction, and at least he stuck his tail on the donkey — right on his head. Janey and I laughed.

"Ouch!" said a gruff voice. "That's a silly place for a tail."

"Who said that?" yelled Petey, tearing off the blindfold.

"Said what, Petey?" asked Mr. Pudgins.

" 'Ouch'. Somebody said 'ouch'!"

"Oh, you're just imagining things," I answered. "It's

Janey's turn now." Janey had a blindfold put on, whirled around three times, and set off for the donkey. She was lucky and pinned her tail on the back end.

"That's better," a gruff voice whispered.

"Oh, is it?" asked Janey.

"You peeked," said Pete.

"I did not," snapped Janey.

"All right, all right," said Mr. Pudgins. "It's Johnny's turn." So I put on the blindfold, took the tail and pin, and whirled around. It was a funny, dizzy feeling, and I wondered where I was. Right then I ran into the donkey. He didn't feel like paper at all. I stuck my pin in and forgot everything trying to get the blindfold off.

I could hear Janey and Pete laughing.

"Well, really!"

Yes, somebody had said that.

"On his tummy, you've got it on his tummy," laughed Petey.

"He looks funny," said Janey.

"Now it's my turn," said Mr. Pudgins. We had a struggle getting the blindfold on him, and he was awfully hard to turn around. Finally, he started off toward the donkey, and we all laughed when he pinned it on the donkey's chin. It looked like a beard.

"Really, that is the last straw." There was that voice again.

"I heard it. I heard it," yelled Petey.

"Me too," said Janey. "There's somebody else here."

"Maybe so," I said. "But where?"

"Right here of course, stupid!" said the same gruff and sad voice. "On the wall."

We could hardly believe our ears, but yes, it was the donkey talking. "One would think," the donkey continued, "that a grown man could do better than pin a tail on a chin. It's all out of place."

"Now, now," said Mr. Pudgins, putting the blindfold on a chair, "it's just a game."

"I'm getting pretty tired of it," said the donkey and walked right off the paper. "Look at me. A tail on my chin, a tail on my head, a tail on my stomach, and a tail where a tail should be. I'm a freak."

"They look handy to me," I said. "You can keep flies off no matter where they are."

"Hummph!" said the donkey. "It's not that I'm complaining. Only I look awfully silly. I think . . . yes, I am. I'm going to cry."

"Quick, before he gets started. Let's play ring-around-the-rosey," said Mr. Pudgins.

I grabbed a head tail, and Janey grabbed the rear tail, and the rest of us joined hands. Around and around we went singing in our loudest voices, and the donkey joined in. Only he went, "He haw . . . he haw." Sometimes when we all fell down, we would just lie and laugh because the donkey looked so funny with his four tails and four legs waving in the air.

Gollee, that game was fun. Finally we were too tired to play any more, and Mr. Pudgins suggested that we should have the ice cream and cake now. When we got to the table, each of us had one of those long crepe-paper snappers at his place. The donkey sat at the head of the table in Dad's place and looked very important. We started to sing "Happy birthday to you" as Mr. Pudgins came through the door with his birthday cake. And then we stopped. Because around the edge of the cake marched twelve little wooden soldiers, and in the very center was a frosting house from which a little girl peeked. We almost thought we could hear her singing "Happy birthday." Believe me, we kept our eyes glued to that wonderful cake. As Mr. Pudgins started to cut

the cake, we got over our surprise enough to really sing, and the donkey joined in with his "He haw" until the dining room rang with sound. Mr. Pudgins smiled.

When we finished eating the ice cream and cake, Mr.

Pudgins said, "Why, we forgot the snappers." And sure enough, we had. So each of us took our red crepe-paper snappers in our hands and pulled on the white tab. Bang! Bang! Bang! I pulled out a jockey cap, Pete found a clown hat in his, and Janey got a flowered dunce cap.

Bang! Mr. Pudgins' snapper finally exploded, and he perched a red bellhop's cap on his head. We giggled. At the other end of the table the donkey was pulling with his chin tail and teeth at his snapper. Bang! Boy, that was a loud one. The donkey went over backward in surprise. With a sad expression he showed us his soldier cap. Janey took it, punched a hole in the top for the head tail to go through, and then placed it on his head between his ears. "Now," said the donkey in a solemn way, "I am the handsomest donkey here." And we agreed he was.

"Look for the favors," said Mr. Pudgins. "There should be favors in those snappers, too."

Janey found hers first. It was a little gold ring that just fit her finger. Petey found a tiny gun that would really shoot water. I had an airplane pin with a propeller that would spin. And Mr. Pudgins had a tiny silver whistle on a chain.

"Oh, what wonderful gifts," sighed Janey.

"Bang, bang," shouted Pete as he squirted us.

"Thanks a lot, Mr. Pudgins," I said, as I pinned the airplane on my shirt.

"I don't suppose," said the donkey's mournful voice, "that I have anything. I never do. And he tugged at his snapper. Whoosh! Something flew out, and it went so fast that for a moment we couldn't see it.

"Why . . . why!" said Janey. "It's an elf."

"My goodness. A tomte," said Mr. Pudgins.

"A what *ee*?" said Pete.

"A tomte," said Mr. Pudgins. "A Scandinavian household elf. Is anyone Swedish here?"

"My mother is," I said.

"Have you ever had an elf before?" asked Mr. Pudgins.

"I don't think so," said Janey, hesitatingly.

The elf was sitting on Mr. Pudgins' water glass, kicking his heels. "High time, I'd say," came a little voice, "that they got one."

"Is he a good elf?" asked Pete.

"Why, of course," said the elf. "But only as long as you are good. When the children in the house are naughty, I'm naughty too. Otherwise I look after you and keep you all happy and pleasant."

"I don't think my mother is going to like him," I said. "She doesn't hold with elves and fairies."

"Well, after all," said the donkey almost crying. "He is my present. I want my present." And then he began to "He haw" so loudly that he blew us right into the living room.

"Perhaps we can catch the tomte," I suggested. And we did try. We chased that elf over the chairs, up on the drapes, across the bookshelves. But he was never there when we grabbed. Mr. Pudgins just sat down in his chair and laughed at us. I guess we did look pretty silly. Finally we gave up, and the tomte giggled and hooted at us from the molding. "I've come to stay," he called in a tinkly voice. "Remember to be kind and helpful, or I'll be naughty too." And then whoof, he disappeared!

"I want my present," yowled the donkey. "He haw . . . he haw."

"Here, here," said Mr. Pudgins, "take mine." And he handed the donkey his silver whistle.

"Whatever use is that?" mourned the donkey.

"Look," said Janey, "I'll put a ribbon through the chain, and you can tie it round your neck. You certainly *are* the handsomest donkey here now."

"So I am," said the donkey, modestly. Then he blew a tiny toot on his whistle.

"Time for bed," said Mr. Pudgins.

We knew there was no point in arguing. It just did no good with Mr. Pudgins, so we quickly trooped off. It had been a wonderful party. And to think we had a tomte! That was pretty exciting. As we fell asleep, we could hear the distant sounds of the little whistle.

In the morning the donkey and Mr. Pudgins were both gone when we got downstairs. We were all a little tired and cross from the excitement the night before. Petey hit Jane for knocking over his blocks, and then I got into the squabble by spanking Pete, who kicked and hit at me. Janey screamed for Mother. She was exasperated with us and made us each sit in a chair, facing the wall.

Then from the kitchen we heard more exasperated sounds. "Oh dear, what is the matter this morning?" said Mother. "Just everything is going wrong. I reached for the oatmeal, and the Cream of Wheat tipped over into the silver drawer. I pulled out the drawer to wipe it, and the whole thing fell on the floor. Oh, dear."

We all looked at each other. We knew who that was. It was the tomte doing all that mischief.

"Father, come help," called Mother. "Now I've spilled the milk!"

We didn't tell Mother about the tomte, but ever after

that when we were cross and unkind, things fell from shelves, doors banged, and bottles broke. But when we were good, the whole house seemed to sing with happiness. Yes, a tomte was worth the trouble.

12. The Christmas Tree

DAD WAS ALL DRESSED up in a Santa Claus suit, and Mother was standing back a way looking at him.

"No, you need more stomach," said Mother.

"Not another pillow," moaned Dad. "I'm so loaded that I can hardly move."

"Will you shake like a bowlful of jelly?" asked Pete.

"More like a sackful of pillows, I'm thinking," said Dad. "Oho . . . ohohoho," he roared. "Hey, cut out the tickling, John."

"Okay. But it really is a pretty good effect," I said. "You laugh pretty well."

"Here, Jack, stick this in." Mother handed Dad another sofa pillow.

Dad shoved the pillow under his belt. "Frankly," he said, "I'm going to look more like an ad for overstuffed furniture than Santa Claus if you keep this up."

"Dear me, look at the time! Did I hear Mr. Pudgins' car?" said Mother.

"Yep! Here he comes," yelled Pete.

Mr. Pudgins and Dad met at the door, and we kids just roared as they tried to go through together. Both were so plump. They got stuck.

"Excuse me," said Mr. Pudgins, stepping back.

"Sorry," gruffed Dad, stepping back in the house. "You first, sir," he said, sweeping low with his red Santa Claus hat.

"No, no, you go first," insisted Mr. Pudgins.

Then they both stepped forward and tried to get through the door at the same time. Now they were really stuck. Wedged tight.

"Jack, please, stop this nonsense," said Mother. She shoved at Dad, and I shoved on her, and we pushed Dad right through the door. We were pushing so hard that all three of us landed in a heap in the snowbank outside the door.

"Humph!" said Dad. "Fine way to treat Santa Claus." But we could see that he was having fun.

"Put on a good show for those orphan kids," I yelled. Pete and Janey were squealing with laughter and scattering snow in the air as the car left. Mother waved to us until the car disappeared.

Mr. Pudgins was sitting in the big armchair, smoking his pipe and watching the fire. I was glad to see that pipe. Maybe tonight would be another of those exciting times. As a special favor, Mother had allowed us a log fire. After all, it was almost Christmas, and the flames did make the room cozy and festive.

Every few minutes Pete ran to the window, pressed his nose against the glass, and crooned, "It's snowing. It's snowing." Peter was eager to have plenty of snow for Santa's sleigh.

"Only three more days till Christmas," sighed Janey. "I wish it were here now."

"Me too," chimed in Pete. "I wanta decorate the tree. Can't we, Johnny?"

"Now look here, kids," I said. "You know what a fuss Mom made about even setting up the tree. She likes to wait until Christmas Eve. And we promised not to nag her about decorating it now. Gosh, it does make the house Christmasy! Smell?"

We all sniffed the air.

"Perhaps we could decorate the tree, Johnny."

"But, Mr. Pudgins . . ."

"If we made our own decorations."

"Please, please, Johnny. Let's." Janey was excited.

"Well, all right," I said grudgingly. "Maybe if we made them."

"Let's start right now," said Janey. She was all set to go.

"What'll we make them of?" asked Pete. He sat down with his scissors.

"What about paper?" suggested Mr. Pudgins.

"Too much mess," I said rather shortly.

"Popcorn?" Mr. Pudgins looked at me inquiringly.

"Naaaah!" I was in a bad mood.

"Well . . ." Mr. Pudgins looked very thoughtful. "Perhaps I could blow a few."

"Will you? Oh, will you?" squealed Janey.

That sounded pretty interesting even to me. "What will you blow them with?" I asked.

"With my pipe, of course," said Mr. Pudgins. And he leaned back in his chair, ready to start. "I warn you, though, they won't last." Slowly he started to puff. And out from the bowl of his pipe came a small smoke ball. It grew and grew until it was just the right size for the tree, and then it floated off from his pipe. I grabbed and missed. Pete grabbed and missed. But Janey jumped onto the davenport and caught it.

"Gently now, my girl," said Mr. Pudgins.

And Jane carefully brought the ball to us. I glanced at it just casually. It was grayish transparent stuff. Then I gasped. For there on the inside were all of us and Mr. Pudgins. We were sitting in Annabelle way up on the coal truck. And when you moved the ball, the truck bounced and moved about.

"Oh," sighed Jane. "What a wonderful ball!" And she hung it very carefully on the tree halfway up.

Now from the pipe came a reddish smoke, and it bulged into a pear-shaped ball. I caught this one just as it broke loose from the pipe. Jane and Pete crowded round. We peered into the pinky stuff and there . . .

"Oh, look! See us in the bathtub," giggled Petey. And we all started to laugh, for we could well remember the fun of the night the bathtub floated. "This one goes up very high," I said. "It's special."

"Me next," called Pete. He ran back to Mr. Pudgins and watched a yellow football shape take form. He grabbed as it floated past him, but he missed. Round and round the room he ran chasing his ball. It drifted always ahead of him.

"You're making such a breeze," suggested Mr. Pudgins, "that the ball can't settle. Why don't you sit down for a moment?"

Pete perched on the edge of a chair, and so did the rest of us. Lower and lower came the ball and very gently eased onto Pete's head. He got slightly frantic because he couldn't see to get the ball and was afraid he might smash it. Janey hopped up, picked the ball off his head, and handed it to him. Then we all looked. There was our lemonade stand with Pete and Janey, slightly purple, standing beside me as we sold the elegant pop that ran from our faucets. Pete hated to hang that ball on the tree. It was such fun to jiggle the ball and watch the little figures move, especially since they were us.

We looked so long that a pure white ball floated off before we got back to Mr. Pudgins. We couldn't catch it. We tried sitting, but it just wouldn't come down. We gave up and watched a green bumpy caterpillar ball

blow up, and, believe me, I took hold before this one could drift away. And there were the mirror children and us staring at each other. Janey gave them a shake to make them all dance.

"Weren't they fun?" sighed Janey.

I knew just how she felt. It was fun to remember our good times, but I felt a little sad, too. I hung that ball where Petey could watch the figures.

"There's that darn white ball again," I muttered, watching it trying to land near Mr. Pudgins' head. Then I forgot it when I saw the delicate blue ball floating in Jane's hand. We peered in and laughed as we

saw the whole birthday party again. How that donkey
was he-hawing, and if we were very quiet, we could
hear his faint "He haw."

"Oh, the darling," murmured Jane. "Aren't these just
perfect balls?"

I nodded and turned to see Mr. Pudgins brushing off
the white ball from his ear. "Bouncing butterballs," he
muttered. "Wish that thing wouldn't keep pestering
me." Now an orange ball broke loose, and Pete caught
it with a whoop. "I've got it! I've got it!" he yelled. "Oh,
it's the train. The wonderful train." And we all listened
for a faint whistle. Yes, there it was.

Now Janey grabbed and held a lavender cylinder
and almost cooed over it. For all the little animals from

the circus — Podo as a clown, the rabbits, the little mice and kittens, why, even the skunks — were caught inside it. A jounce of the ball, and they wiggled around.

"If this ball!" Mr. Pudgins was really exasperated. He brushed away the white ball which was tickling his ear. From his pipe bowl rose a green and yellow ball. I snatched it, and we could hear birds even before we looked inside. Yes, there they were — our Whizzle birds. They were flying round and round, and three little children were chasing them.

Now we stood back for a moment and looked at the tree. The balls glowed slightly in their different colors, and we could just make out the scenes inside them.

"Oh, Mr. Pudgins, do blow one of you now," said Janey.

"One of me?" He sounded surprised.

"Yes, a special one to keep," she said.

"Well . . ." He seemed to be considering the situation. And then the white ball bounced on his head, down his nose, past his chin, and back up to his eyes.

"This dratted ball," growled Mr. Pudgins. "I didn't even think this one up, and now it's pestering me. Pestering me? I wonder." Gently he took it in his hand and looked inside. "Oh my! Dear me!" he murmured.

We leaned over the ball too, and there inside was another scene, but not of our happy times. A little girl was sitting beside a still smaller boy lying on a bed. He looked sick. Mr. Pudgins held the ball to his ear and

listened. "I must go!" He said it so firmly that my heart jumped. I thought he'd leave right that minute.

"Don't look so worried, kiddies." He smiled. "I will wait until morning. But I just heard Betty. . . . Can you see her in here?"

We all nodded. "She's trying to play with Tim and amuse him. But Tim keeps saying, 'Six months in bed. Oh, Betty . . . !'" We looked in the ball, and we could see him sobbing. "So I must go," continued Mr. Pudgins. "I am needed there. And after all, you are getting pretty old for a babysitter."

He was right about that, too. Mother had been slightly provoked the last few times at our insisting on having Mr. Pudgins, for she thought we could stay alone.

"I always keep in touch with you with these smoke balls so I am never far away. If you need me, I will know."

"But it's Christmas," said Janey and started to cry. "It won't seem like Christmas with you gone away."

I could feel a lump rising in my throat, too. I choked it back. I was too big to cry.

"Don't go, Mr. Pudgins," sobbed Petey.

"I am sorry, lad, but I must. However, I shall leave a very special ball for you. After you are in bed, I will blow it, and this one will last. Shall we play some Christmas music on the phonograph?" he asked.

"Yes! Yes!" we all shouted.

It was so peaceful to sit and watch the dancing balls while a choir sang lovely Christmas songs. It was as if the loveliness soaked right into us. Quietly Mr. Pudgins' voice said, as we shut off the last record, "Bedtime now. And I will remember your ball."

We trudged off sadly, although we were a little heartened by the thought that Mr. Pudgins could always check on us through his own special television. It gave you a cozy feeling.

The next morning Mother was a little surprised that we jumped out of bed so quickly and raced for the tree.

The balls were all gone, though here and there on the tree was a little touch of color where they had hung. Then, at the very top, we spied a silvery ball. It seemed to shimmer. We gasped. "Oh yes," said Mother, "Mr. Pudgins left that for you children. It is lovely, isn't it?"

She let me hold it for a minute, and as I looked in it, I could see Mr. Pudgins riding along in Annabelle with Podo beside him. He waved.

"Can you see it? The picture?" I asked.

From Mother's surprised expression, I knew she couldn't so I let the matter drop. But Jane and Pete could.

"Hi," said Pete.

"Good-bye, Mr. Pudgins. Good-bye," I murmured.

"Come back. Come back sometimes," called Janey.

And I think — yes, I know — that Mr. Pudgins nodded his head and smiled.